TRIPLE TIME

DRUE HEINZ LITERATURE PRIZE 2009

TRIPLE TIME

ANNE SANOW

UNIVERSITY OF PITTSBURGH PRESS

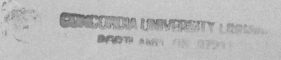

Published by the University of Pittsburgh Press, Pittsburgh, Pa., 15260

Copyright © 2009, Anne Sanow

Manufactured in the United States of America

Printed on acid-free paper

10 9 8 7 6 5 4 3 2 1

Library of Congress Cataloging-in-Publication Data

Sanow, Anne.

Triple time / Anne Sanow.

p. cm. — (Drue Heinz literature prize)

Includes bibliographical references.

ISBN-13: 978-0-8229-4380-8 (cloth : alk. paper)

ISBN-10: 0-8229-4380-8 (cloth : alk. paper)

1. Middle East—Fiction. 2. Americans—Middle East—Fiction. I. Title.

PS3619.A5673T75 2009

813'.6—dc22

2009013155

For Bob and Vicki

and in memory of Jane Sawyer

Oh, a heartstopper is the solitaire's one note—high, sweet, lonely, magic.

Jean Rhys, *Wide Sargasso Sea*

CONTENTS

TRIPLE TIME

PIONEER

Up in the cliffs, protruding from a crevice no wider than a plywood board, there is a tail, maybe a goat's, flicking up and down again. There's a suspension of movement and then the animal backs up, defecating. Chris rests his nose against the fence to keep his sightline level; the goat continues to scrabble and root while its excrement drops behind it, turning the same baked yellow as the escarpments. It's that hot. The goats will eat nearly anything and they are adroit, vertical climbers—and here just across the road from the building site it's feastland, a cornucopia of discarded food containers, insulation strips, chunks of wood and plaster, and tin cans, which in accordance with all mythology they gnaw vigorously. Wild dogs assist by messing about in the garbage at night and distributing it on the road. Over the past weeks Chris has seen the goats become fatter, roly-bellied and tottering, and each morning as he rides out in the truck he sees them ambling about the mosque in the village, their side-planted eyes following him as he passes, mouths chewing in mockery or greeting.

The village is the sentry to the Wadi Laban. At least this is how Chris, who is nine, sees it: the road from the city passes down the chute of the canyon, and then there is the sharp brow of rocks straight ahead. A cluster of mud houses and some palms sprout from seemingly nothing. To the left is a narrow path for men and goats, and the only way for a car or truck to proceed is to the right, down the new paved road that winds one mile to the place where Chris's father is supervising the building of a housing compound. The turn past the village is sharp and precise, and there is always someone watching them drive by. Usually it is the old man who owns the small grocery. Chris's father often stops there, leaving the truck idling, and buys gallon jugs of purified water for the men at the site and sticky cans of sweet Vimto soda for Chris. When Chris's father goes in the store he says to the shop owner *salaam alaykum* or *alaykum salaam*, depending on who has initiated the greeting. At the building site, he jokes with the other Americans who have dubbed the village B-1; the future government compound has already been designated B-2 by some people back in Washington, and the workers are behind schedule in completing it.

It's some strange trick of time but in the month that he has been spending in this place, Chris is never bored. They are long days, too, and because it is July they begin early, with the sun gleaming from the horizon at five and pulsing with full force by eight-thirty or nine. It will be a hundred and ten, a hundred and twenty degrees; at least it isn't humid, Chris's mother says, like it would be if they were stationed in Jeddah, which is on the Red Sea. Chris can't imagine what the Red Sea might look like. For now he is obsessed with his waiting game, in which he holds himself rigid for hours like a stalker. His efforts pay off and he keeps a tally of the goats and lizards he spots every day, and he hopes for additional wriggles or thrashings in the craggy rocks, anything he can study and fix on so that he can learn its movements and habits.

"That shit'll be all over the fucking road again," says a voice behind him. Chris jumps, then relaxes. It's Radi, whose mimicry of the tough-talking Americans is made comical in his clear, flutish voice.

"Yeah," Chris agrees, watching as Radi hops up onto a rock next to him, flipping his ghotra back from his headband to look through the fence.

"*Yeah,*" Radi says, drawling it out. Sometimes he just repeats words and inflections, and he remembers them all; other times, Chris can't be sure that there isn't a mean streak in him, an older boy's hazing reflex. Radi is fourteen. Instead of joining the Saudi National Guard this summer he works on the site, organizing tools and supplies.

"Want to shoot?" Radi asks. He aims up into the rocks, *psh psh.* "Think your dad will let you?"

"Maybe," Chris says. Not that his father ever has.

Radi's eyes widen. "No shit?"

"We have a gun at home."

At this Radi laughs. "Ah, *we* have a gun. I see. No, I think it is your *father's.* Yes? You're too young." He steps off the rock. "Come on. I'm here to get you."

Chris gets down from the fence and follows Radi. It's useless, Radi doesn't take him seriously, but Chris says, "My father was in Vietnam." Radi slows a bit and smiles, and for a moment, facing Chris, he looks malevolent. Maybe it's the sun, backlighting his white thobe so that it looks flamed around the outline of his body. But then he waits until Chris catches up and says, "Maybe I'll show you *my* father's gun. He was in a war too. Okay?"

"Okay," says Chris. He doesn't want to admit that he does not know which war Radi means.

They go into a white tent where Chris's father and his fellow engineers are unpacking lunch from big coolers brought in by some Yemeni boys. The ice in the bottom of the coolers has gone to slush. "Look sharp," Chris's father calls to him, lobbing a sandwich. Chris catches it, low at the waist. It's soggy in the wrapper, probably salami and weird German cheese. Never ham. "Radi?" his father says, gesturing. But Radi signals no with a palm and backs out, casually, like he has somewhere else he needs to be.

"Masalaam'," he says. He taps Chris on the shoulder as he goes.

"Masa*later*," one of the engineers calls back. Chris's father offers Radi a sandwich every day; he never takes it. Sometimes he eats with the laborers, or he goes back to the little family farm a few miles down the road. Either way, they won't see him again until after noon prayer.

Chris's father sits next to him on the floor of the tent, which is covered with dusty rugs. He wipes some of the reddish sand from his sunburned forehead. "So," he says, "how's the Great Laban Wildlife Survey?"

"There are two kinds of goats," Chris says, all seriousness. "Those ones we see all the time, and then these smaller ones, with different horns. They're like antelope."

"Okay," his father says. "We'll have to check that out." He's tired, Chris can tell. This work is not difficult for him—he's always worked long hours, as far as Chris can remember it, but now they need more money and Chris's mother waits for them each day back at the house. It all seems to be making his father look older than he should, but he's trying. He's pleasant around the other men but quieter, more controlled.

"Hey, Chris," one of the men says from the other side of the tent. His accent is one target for Radi's imitations: words coming out with a hard twang. "How do you feel about getting a baby sister?"

Chris shrugs, watching his father. "It's okay," he says.

"Gives your mother something to do, that's for sure." The men who are married agree; the wives are at home all day with no jobs and no cars. Chris has heard his mother complain that she isn't allowed to drive here.

Someone else says, "Well, if you gotta bring 'em with you, you know it's best you just keep them knocked up—"

"Keep them *happy*," the first engineer says, winking at Chris. "*Inshallah*, right? God willing." The other guy looks at Chris's father and says, "Sorry, Mike." His father nods.

"Good timing though, yeah? Just when you get here."

Chris's father joins in the laughter this time. "What are you supposed to do?" he says.

—

There's not much happening after the food; prayer call has wavered over them from the village mosque, and the workers will pray and then rest for an hour. They stay inside the tent for a while, out of the sun. Chris looks at the blueprints his father is explaining to another man—No, the guard gate needs to go *here,* he says, so they can't see over to the swimming pool—and occasionally his father looks over at him. "That's right, isn't it?" It's a new thing for Chris, the first time he's been included this way, and he feels like he's a lot older than he was two months ago, back home.

When prayer ends Chris plays backgammon with the old men from the date farm, who move with the shade every afternoon, tracing the periphery of the site. One of them can say "okay," which he does every time Chris makes a move that is right, or he'll shake his head with a sharp "*la, la!*" and point to the mark that would have been better. The others speak in Arabic but they are all mostly quiet, sipping sweet tea from little glass cups and leaning back with rolled-up rugs under their haunches.

Chris is thinking out his next move when they hear the shout. It comes from the direction of the site, and Chris feels suddenly cold all over. He runs back to where the tallest building—the unfinished prefab concrete of a two-story house—is surrounded by the laborers and the engineers. Chris doesn't think anyone could be hurt too bad from falling, it's not that far, but he looks for his father anxiously. He sees him kneeling over a broken concrete slab, and under the slab is Radi's leg. Radi is stretched out and staring at it, eyes wide, but he is not making a sound.

There's a sharp disagreement of voices, made cacophonous by the wadi's echo. "Dad," Chris says. He comes up behind him. Radi starts to hyperventilate, and Chris's father tells him, "Easy, easy, okay? Don't try to move."

"Get back here," one of the engineers says, guiding Chris away. "We're going to lift that off." One of the laborers, breaking out of the group, goes over to Radi and says something. Radi nods, eyes closed now. "*Hinna, hinna!*" the man says, and other men come over to help. When the slab is pulled away Radi does scream, a high, strangled sound. From where he stands Chris can see dark wet stains where the thobe sticks to his leg. "Okay, okay," Chris's father is saying. Someone brings a first-aid kit and takes out bandages. "No, fuck, that is *not* it," Chris hears his father say. "That's all we've got?"

As Chris stands watching he sees a look that he's seen on his father's face before, that quick fall into frustration, something that melts down. Sometimes Chris thinks that his father spends most of his time inside himself making sure that the look doesn't get out. It happened when he told them that they were going to Saudi Arabia. I don't *have* a job here, Jenny, he'd said to Chris's mother. Two or three years, okay? An adventure, hey Chris? You'll go to school there. There's a bunch of other kids coming too.

Now his father gets it back together. He waves Chris over. Radi's leg is wrapped and splinted, he's stopped groaning but Chris can see he doesn't feel good. He manages a weak grin. "Hey, *sadiq*," he says to Chris.

Chris high-fives him—this, at least, is something he's taught to Radi, who's just called him *friend*. "Are you going to the hospital?" Chris asks. The men have a wheelbarrow, and Radi eyes it.

"Later," he says, waving a hand. Chris looks at his father, whose mouth is a line.

"He's going home first," he says. "Then he's going. But we're gonna see you, right, Radi? We'll come check you out when you're all set up."

Chris knows that Radi's leg must be crushed—there's no way it couldn't be, under the heavy concrete. "We should take him now, Dad," he says. "In our truck." Radi watches him. The men with the wheelbarrow are arguing with one another, and Chris can't understand what they're saying.

"His brother will take him," his father says, with finality.

"But Dad—"

Radi looks away. "Later," he says again, wincing as he gets lifted into the wheelbarrow, splinted leg straight out in front. "You come see me, okay?" The men kick up dust in their hurry to get him down the road.

—

"Linda Garcia told me it happens all the time," his mother says. "Rich has a couple of guys out on his site with permanent limps." She seems to float in the tiny kitchen, a light blue butterfly or bird with a round stomach. After the days out in the baked earth, where everything is pounded by the glare, Chris can't bring her into focus.

"I'm following it up," his father says, head in his hands at the table. "We promised to go see him."

"We?"

"I'm going too," Chris says. He's worried, now, that Radi's leg won't be all right. His father explains that Radi's family won't let their son go to a hospital with strangers; they want to see him themselves, and then decide what to do. "We have to respect that," he says.

"Oh, baby, he'll be okay," his mother says. She smiles at Chris. "We'll all go see him when he gets to the hospital, and after the baby's born you can have Radi come over here to visit, all right?" She's breezy this evening, hummingly cheerful. Chris ducks as she comes by with a plate.

They eat at the card table that is shoved into a corner next to the refrigerator. It's warm there, and the air conditioner wheezes and spits. The house is slapped up from cheap wood and tin, one of forty in neat rows, surrounded by walls. A chain-link fence bars the entry; a boy Radi's age stands guard, holding an automatic rifle. There's nowhere to go except a playground with monkey bars and a slide, which Chris disdains, and is anyway impossible in the heat of the day. He has seen only younger children on the compound so far, no one really his age. His father says they will come when school starts. His mother has made one friend, Linda, whose husband works on another building site. The two women spend their days indoors with the shades drawn, drinking iced tea and making baby clothes.

Chris and his father watch her. She's talking about the Bedouin spice sellers, how they came to the compound with their trucks and camels and were almost turned away by the guard, but then she and the other women banged on the gates and the nomads just pushed right by him. "The poor boy didn't know what to do," she says. "I don't think he has a clue with that gun."

"Which is what I'm afraid of, Jen."

"What, that you'll come home some day and find us all carried off somewhere?" She laughs, but it sounds cracked. Before his father can speak up again she goes on: "I got turmeric, marjoram, some ochre-colored stuff—I don't know the name, but it smells heavenly . . ."

"Did you have an abayah on?" Chris's father interrupts. He looks at her stomach, pushing up the hem of her long Indian dress so that only the back of it brushes the floor.

"Oh, honey," she says. "Don't worry about *me*." She sounds light again, but Chris is on the alert. She was like this when she announced she was pregnant, telling Chris and his father together. What do you think? she'd asked Chris. We're going to Arabia and you're going to get a baby sister.

His father was surprised. Then he asked why she thought it was a girl. I just do, she said.

"Okay, Jen," his father says now. His voice is gentler. She looks away into the kitchen, her fork in the air. "Mom," Chris says, "I want to go see Radi tomorrow." She turns to him slowly with a polite smile. "Oh," she says.

"*Mom*," Chris says, and his father says her name again, but she trills at their joint tone of concern. "Lighten up, you two," she says.

———

Chris awakes to familiar sounds: he can hear his parents' bed, in the room across from his, creak in its metal frame. He knows his

8

father is getting up when the springs give a quick shriek. Then there will be a long grind as his mother rolls over, and a see-saw melody as she balances on the edge. He listens and thinks: *five minutes.* While he tries to move from his own cot—it's Army-issue, and the mattress is blue-striped and thin—he holds his breath as he lies on his back, carefully sliding his legs over.

The bed groans anyway, so he gives up and puts his feet on the floor. A sticker on the mirror over the dresser points a green arrow in the direction of Mecca. In the next room he hears a long sigh and more protests from the springs. *Ow,* his mother says.

In the kitchen Chris finds a lizard on the wall and picks it up by the tail. The tip of it comes off and jerks for a moment in his fingers. "Chris!" his father calls. The lizard skitters under the counter.

"I need you to stay at home today," his father says. He's standing in the doorway, combing wet hair back from his forehead.

"But I thought we were going to see Radi."

"We will. Not today, though. Your mother's not feeling well."

Chris says, "So what?"

"Don't give me that," his father says. He doesn't say anything else as he starts up some water on the stove for coffee. Chris wants to protest: an entire day at home, where he will have little to do; their shipment of household goods has not yet arrived and he has no toys except for the case of Matchbox cars he brought on the plane. But his father looks at him and demands, "Well?" and Chris knows that however they are on their days together on the building site, it is not how they are here.

"Okay," Chris mumbles. He doesn't offer an apology, but his father seems satisfied.

After his father leaves Chris listens for sounds from the bedroom. Deciding that his mother must still be asleep, he goes outside.

It is deserted. Each little house is exactly the same—square and white, window screens matted with dead bugs. Curtains are drawn against the sun. All of the cars and trucks are gone. Chris makes his way around the rectangle of the street, dragging his shoes on the asphalt; the noise seems to get sucked up into the air. Finally, he sees someone: at the end of the block, where tired palm trees make a thin shade over the picnic tables, there is a girl sitting Indian-style with a book and crayons.

She stops what she's doing and looks up at Chris as he comes near. "What are you staring at?" she says to him.

"I'm just walking around," he says. He hasn't seen her before; her blonde hair is cut in feathers, and she has bright blue shadow smeared inexpertly on her eyelids. Her pale arms and legs poke out from cutoff denim shorts and a T-shirt printed with daisies. She must be new here, Chris thinks—certainly she's pretending not to be miserable, just as he is.

When he walks over to the table and sits down, he can see that her face is young and chubby. But when he tells her his name she says, in a mean tone, "Well isn't that nice," like she's trying out something from someone older. She folds her hands over her coloring book, but not before Chris sneaks a look at it: *Charlie's Angels.* She's been coloring Farrah Fawcett's hair, mixing different shades of yellow.

"Forget you," Chris says, getting up to leave. This is the last thing he needs, he thinks—this girl shouldn't talk to him like she's his babysitter. He shoves his hand into his pocket and takes out a Matchbox car.

"Oh, wait. I didn't mean it," she says. "You can sit here if you want to."

"I don't care."

She says, "You have to do something, you know." When she narrows her eyes at him he can see the crease where her eye shadow is melting.

Chris watches her for a few minutes. The only thing she says for a while is that he can't put his car near her book, but this time she sounds conciliatory. Finally he asks her if she is new here, but she says, "No." When they keep talking it's strange: they trade little bits of information, where they're from and how old, and to Chris it seems like a different kind of conversation than he's ever had with anyone his age. It seems like it goes on and on. She hardly looks at him, just concentrating on her coloring and putting the crayons back one by one as she finishes with them.

Then she stands up. "I have to get home or I'll get killed," she says.

Chris shrugs at this abrupt dismissal. "See you," he says. He still doesn't know her name.

As she's walking off she turns around and says to him, "Your mother's having a baby. I know all about it." She hugs her book to her chest like she's protecting herself from a chill, even though the sun is directly over them now. "You don't know how *stupid* that is, do you? Everyone says so."

Chris doesn't know what she means, not exactly, but he doesn't want her telling him anything. The girl stands there, clearly waiting for his reaction. "Shut up," he says finally. It isn't as forceful as he wants it to be.

"I'm just saying," she retorts, haughty. Two more steps away and Chris yells after her, angry now. "Why don't you go home to your *mother*," he says. It's something he's heard before, and right now it's the worst thing he can think of to insult her with.

"She's not my *mother!*" the girl says. She stalks off to the house across the street. With a flush, Chris thinks: that worked.

—

That night Chris sits in his room while his parents talk with the Garcias, who have come over for dinner. The house smells like the spices that Linda Garcia helped his mother mix into the beef-noodle casserole. Now they are drinking beer with ice, which Rich Garcia says tastes better with home brew. They've been here for a year already, making them old hands—their voices are the ones that predominate from the living room, telling stories and insisting that soon enough, this will begin to seem like home.

"In fact, you won't *want* to go back," Linda is saying. "Just wait until summer's over—it's the worst time, everyone gone. After Labor Day there's the ladies' club again and you'll be so busy the days will just *zip* by. Trust me."

Chris's mother says, "Well, but the baby—"

"Oh, don't worry about that. You can always get a part-time nanny."

Chris hears his father mumble something about money, what they can afford, and the two conversations diverge while the men talk about work and the women are quieter. Then Chris hears Linda coming down the hall toward his room, where the bathroom is. "I'll ask the gardener's wife for you," she calls back. "I'm sure she has a sister, or a cousin or something. They all do." As she pushes into the bathroom her long, brightly patterned skirt flares out and she seems to bulk there for a minute until she gets the door open.

It's been the longest day Chris has ever known.

He's examining the property cards from a Monopoly game—Linda brought it over for him, saying that since her kids were still in the States with their grandparents, he might as well have it. He can't play against himself, but he reasons that at least he can memorize what the cards say. He's trying not to be bored.

When the rain starts it hits the roof as loud as bullets. Everyone in the house exclaims—the storm has come up without their noticing it. Out of the bedroom window Chris can see that the sky has gone darker, but it does not look like any storm he's ever seen. The wind is hurling sand. When the rain pelts down it is reddish brown, and it splats against the window so that he can barely see out. All of a sudden it seems cooler.

It's loud, with the rattling sound of the rain, and Chris finds it easy to walk right past the adults, who are now milling about in the kitchen opening and closing cabinets, like they're preparing for something. "Flashlight," Chris's mother says, giggling as she rustles through a drawer. Linda moves to help her, saying, "You always want to—" but Chris's father cuts her off: "Jen, I've told you." He slams the drawer shut and reaches under the sink.

Chris goes out the front door, closing it quietly. It's like he's in a different world, and it is wonderful: the sky is still light in the spaces where there are no clouds, and the mud-rain is orangey now, spewing from the gutters and snaking down the white of the little houses like fiendish tails. His arms and face are getting covered too, and even though it stings when it hits it also feels soft and warmish when it runs off. The street has become a small river. The water swirls around the tires of the cars parked next to each house; it's like they're all floating. Chris takes long strides down the street as if skating. He's almost surprised to feel the drag of his sneakers on the concrete underneath.

Sloshing to the end of the block—the muddiness covers the street so that he can barely see it, and he's pretending that he can walk on water—he stops at the picnic tables by the playground. Across the street is the house the girl went into earlier. The curtains are closed but the house glows. Chris sees a bicycle in the driveway, pushed over by the wind.

There's no one else outside.

For a moment he considers taking the bike. But what would he do with it? He could wheel it over to the playground and leave it there, but it would hardly get any wetter and dirtier than it is already. Also, he thinks, he would be blamed for moving it. He could still do it, though—it would be something to do, something more than he's doing. Things come to his mind as he stands there getting wet: the bike, the girl, the goats out in the wadi by the building site; the Garcias and his parents, who talk at one another and at him, but seem to be speaking another language; the wall at the end of the street that he can't see through; Radi and his broken leg, which everyone seems to have forgotten about. He's not sure which of these things make any sense, or why they're all in his mind together.

In the end he doesn't take the bike. When he comes home he feels like he's been gone for hours, but his mother merely looks up from the couch where she's still talking with Linda and says, "Oh, you went out?" She puts her hands on her stomach and smiles. "He's probably all wet," she continues, but she's not looking at Chris as he drips his way down the hall and back to his room.

———

The storm has dried up entirely by the next morning, but it has left swaths of red mud that streak across the roads. Out at the site, the men have knocked down the frame of the house that fell and are going to start again. Chris sorts Radi's tools. "They'll do it," one of the engineers says, gesturing impatiently to the laborers, but Chris's father says, "No, let him." "Fine," the engineer says, and backs off. Chris's father looks down at him, frowning. "You okay there?" Chris nods. He organizes by size and type, standing the large axes and shovels against a wall.

Chris is glad he's been allowed to come out again today with his father—*Bye now*, his mother waved them off this morning, distracted. Here, at least, he has a task. It seems important to complete it before searching for more animals; there has been no word about Radi, but Chris wants to have his things ready for him.

A truck careens through the gate, billowing sand. Chris sees that it's the gardener from their neighborhood, yelling and waving at them through the window. "Dad," he says, standing. His father looks up. They both know.

They can see nothing but stillness when they get back to the house. This frightens Chris; there should be activity, people should be doing things, like the gardener who came out to get them. He led the way back, leaning on his horn down the highway and clearing the way for Chris and his father to follow.

In the house, though, there's noise. Linda Garcia and some of the other wives are here, filling the kitchen and the bathroom and bringing things into the bedroom. The kitchen table is stacked with pots and pans. One of the women pulls a pair of scissors from a drawer, and then a knife, weighing them in her palms to consider them. Chris's stomach twinges. He hears muted, urgent argument from the bedroom. His mother is saying a lot of things: It's too soon, not yet, it's only eight months, fuck this, I can't believe it. Then she makes a noise that sounds like she's wounded, like Radi when the concrete slab was lifted away.

"I raised Rich on the landline," Linda says to Chris's father, stopping him in the hallway. She checks her watch with a frown. "I'm sorry it took so long; we weren't here, and when we got back from the souks the only line working was the Colonel's—"

14

"All right," Chris's father says. "Jen, it's all right." Chris follows him to the bedroom door. "No, no," Linda says, pulling Chris back out. He sees Maryam, the gardener's wife, squatting on the floor by the bed and holding his mother on her lap. "She knows what she's doing," Linda says. His mother is going to have the baby here, Chris understands, in this hot little house, because the hospital is too far away and they are too late.

"Chris," his father says. He comes back from the hallway to where Chris is standing by the table. "I want you to go over to Colonel Macpherson's and stay there until I get you. Okay?"

"I'll take him," Linda says. Chris shakes off her hand; he's afraid of what will happen when he leaves.

"Chris."

"Yeah." He looks at his father. His face is tighter than when Radi was hurt, his eyes bleak, but steady. "Please," he says to Chris. "Go on. Look—" He sighs, coming over and taking Chris to the window. There are two little kids on tricycles across the street, wearing paper Uncle Sam hats with *1776/1976* in silver glitter on the rims. "It's better for your mother this way. Do you understand?"

"She's going to be okay," Chris says, though he is not certain. "That's right," his father says.

Linda takes Chris three blocks away to the house of Colonel Macpherson and his wife. Their daughter Kimberly is ten years old, Linda tells him. She gives Chris a little pat on the shoulder when he goes in the door. The house is just like his on the outside, but inside there are red rugs on the floor and leafy plants in brass pots clogging the entryway. It is midafternoon but the colonel is home from work. He is a large man, taking up half the couch where he sits next to his wife, who stops talking and glares at him when he gets up to greet Chris.

"There you are," the colonel booms, as if they'd been expecting him for a long time. "Make yourself at home there, Chris. Why don't you go meet Kimberly."

"Okay," Chris says. Neither of the adults moves, so he walks down the hall automatically to the bedroom that's in the same place his is. When he looks in he sees the girl from the playground. She's sitting on the floor next to the bed, wearing bell-bottoms now, and a halter top that cuts into her stomach. Her room is covered with posters. Rainbows, kittens, and *Teen Beat* heartthrobs all blur together in a haze of pink and purple.

"Oh," the girl says. "Hi." She sounds as unsurprised as her father. Glancing through the door, she rolls her eyes in the direction of the living room.

She says that Chris can sit with her in her room if he doesn't bug her. She puts a record on her turntable and when Chris asks what it is she says, "Led Zeppelin." Chris thinks for a moment: he remembers music pounding out from passing cars in his old neighborhood, radiating from open doors and fire escapes of the apartments where they lived, a long time ago, it seems.

"Led Zeppelin is a fag," he says to Kimberly, affecting a knowing tone. She gives him an arch look that scares him; she is, suddenly, discernibly older than he. "Moron," she laughs. She puts on her headphones so that he can't hear the music, and leans against the wall.

Chris leaves her room and sits in the hallway. He pokes angrily at a filmy-legged spider crawling up the wall. It is insulting to be brought here, after everything he has seen and done, after Radi, after his mother. Colonel Mac's wife is talking to her husband in a shrill voice and Chris can hear her easily through the thin walls. "I don't care anymore," he hears her say. "I don't." The Colonel is harder to hear because he slurs, in a much deeper voice, and the ice in his glass is loud like castanets.

———

It's a miracle, his mother likes to say now. Can you believe it? They are home together in the evening, Chris and his mother and his father, and the baby, his new sister Melanie. The gardener's wife has come every day with Linda Garcia for the past three weeks. When Chris and his father come home it is Linda who shoos them to the table to eat. "Now don't you be doing the dishes," she says to Chris's mother as she's leaving. "That's what Maryam's for."

Chris still hasn't seen Radi yet, though they have had vague assurances, from a man claiming to be Radi's uncle, that his broken leg is mending. *La*, the man said when he visited the building site: there was no need for a doctor. He flicked his ghotra back with an unhurried gesture when he spoke with Chris's father. The other engineers stayed away. "He'll be back for money," one of them said later. His father replied that maybe they should just give him some, if that's the way things were done around here. He was angry; tonight, he just seems discouraged. "I don't know if Radi *will* make it back," he says, as he and Chris eat their dinner together.

"What?" his mother asks. She's sitting on the couch, fussing with a laundry basket of cloth diapers, which she complained about having to use because Pampers are too expensive here. But now she seems happy enough. She makes three tufts of white fabric into a stack, smacking it flat. "Who are you talking about, Mike?"

"The Saudi boy," his father says to her. "Chris's friend from the site."

She frowns. "I didn't know that," she says.

"The one who broke his leg, Mom. He's not better yet. I want to go see him." Chris looks at his father; he acknowledges him but also casts a warning glance toward his wife. "I don't know—" she begins, smoothing the diapers and pulling the edges straight. Chris and his father watch her.

"It's okay, Mom," Chris says. All in a rush, he explains that he knows everything on the building site, the date farm next to it, the farmers, and the direction down the road past the escarpments. He has been watching and he remembers the direction Radi walked every day, probably where his family lives, and it would be easy to find if he just walked down the road. If he could see Radi he could make sure that he was feeling all right. It might be better if he went, he says, because it would be okay and Radi's parents would understand. It is the right thing, and it would be better than doing nothing. There is nothing to do on the compound and they know it. He has absorbed something of this other place now, the unmarked edge of what is still foreign to them, and as he tries to explain it he sees his father looking at him the way he sometimes looks at him in certain brief shared moments together out on the site.

Chris stops. He has no idea if he's said anything that he really feels. But the look between him and his father still hangs there across the table.

"What are we doing here," Chris's mother says softly. Chris and his father look up; the plaintive interruption feels expected. Her hands are in her lap, twisted into a clean diaper that is bright as snow. She's had nothing to say, except for the same things over and over again with Linda, how to live here and what that means, and now, Chris sees, she is finally through with it, her effervescence deflated. She's just alone in this place, while Chris and his father are gone. "Is this really going to work out this time, Mike?"

His father doesn't say anything for a moment. "I don't know, honey," he says. "I have no idea, except that I think it will be good. I know that we're a unit, and we're in this together. Okay? All of us." He pushes back from the table to join her on the couch and lets her lean into his arm. "It was just—everything," she says after a minute. "All that." He strokes her hair. "I know, honey," he says. "It was awful. But you're brave, you stuck it."

"Yeah?"

"Yeah." He encircles her, pulls her close.

She doesn't say anything for a moment, resting her head and looking out the living room window. Chris follows her gaze and tries to see what she sees. There is the corner of the Garcia's house, where the sun is hitting metal and flashing as it goes down. The Garcias have a little flag waving from a pole stuck into a window frame, and though the stars and stripes have already faded from the sun, it flips jauntily in the breeze. There's the chain-link fence, and beyond that just hot sky and sand and the city. Somewhere out there is the school he will go to, and other things being built.

"Baby," his mother says to him. She's smiling now, looking content with where she is. "Will you go and look in on your sister? Just a quick look."

"Okay," Chris says. He goes into the bedroom. Melanie is sleeping on her back, making gentle tadpole movements with her legs and wriggling her fingers.

"She's fine, Mom," Chris calls back. "She's good."

"Thanks, baby," his mother replies.

Chris goes over to the crib again and looks at his sister lying there. She's kicked the sheet back and he moves to carefully pull it up again. He doesn't want to wake her because the house is so quiet now. As he tucks it up his hand rests for a moment on her chest; she's heaving snuffy baby sleep, and at his touch she grows calmer. He keeps his hand lightly there for a moment. She's fine now. There is her breath, Chris thinks. There is her breath. There is her heart.

THE DATE FARM

Jill stands a few yards in front of the pickup truck, letting the sand blow around her ankles. All the way out to the desert they'd been racing toward the sunset, and now, at the top of the escarpment, it is about to bleed into the horizon. The sky wipes into navy, a big piece of dark coming down, flecked with stars.

"Oh," she says softly, out over the edge.

Sean calls to her, "Hey, darlin'. You want to do me a favor and come back from the edge a little, okay?" His voice is odd to her yet; he is English, but his accent mingles with twangy inflections he has picked up from the many Americans in Riyadh, people from Texas or the deep South. She cannot make out some of their phrasings herself. She is jarred by them, feeling displaced at parties or in the markets, where a y'all will ping above the guttural Arabic like a honeyed alarm. They are far from the city now, however. She makes a vague reply to assure Sean that she is not so stupid as to fall down the cliff face. She wonders if she would hurt herself falling down; should she miss the cragged rocks, the sand below looks pillowy and soft, almost welcoming.

Sean says something else but the words slip in and out of Jill's earshot with each pulse of wind. She does not bother to turn around. She squats down on her haunches the way the rug sellers do when drinking tea in the souks. Her small frame is lost in the white thobe, which billows out from where it has caught behind her knees, and she has wound a red-checked ghotra tight on her head to cover her hair. That afternoon Sean had told her that no way was he taking her anywhere all got up in that genderfuck outfit. It was the first time she'd heard the word *genderfuck* and she laughed. For the rest of the party she'd sashayed about, her bikini visible through the cloth in flashes of turquoise, and when Sean was the only one still sober enough to drive she figured that he'd take her rather than let her charm one of the other guys into it.

"You're how old again?" he'd asked as they climbed into the truck. It was crusted in hues of umber, splatted designs of mud and sand, as if from a high-pressure paint gun. A weekly hose wash by the houseboy did little to improve it.

"Eighteen," she replied, used to the question.

"Christ. Keep covered up." Before going he insisted that she at least don jeans and a shirt underneath her costume.

"Oh, you knew that," Jill said.

"Well, the last thing I need is to get stopped with some underage chippie playing dress-up in men's clothing. So I'm driving you, but you do what I say out on the road."

"Fine." She pulled the ghotra in around her face, letting the folds shadow the angles of her features. A small flap flickered in time with the breaths from her nose. Although she did not have the traditional black cord to hold the cloth on her head, she looked like a prepubescent boy, maybe the son of a Saudi business owner, being driven by a Western employee.

Sean opened up speed once they were past Intercontinental Road. He gunned it and went straight for the horizon; they passed only a few Mercedes water trucks for nearly an hour. When he pulled off the highway into the dunes (there was a particular point at which to make the turn, past the roadside boulder hugged by the carcass of a long-forgotten crashed limousine), the escarpments rose in front of them. He knew where you could drive right up one of the ridges that was wide and hard enough to hold the truck, and this is where he took her.

Jill can feel him now hesitating, staring at her back, or perhaps into the sky. At this moment she wishes that she could be alone. The very idea of taking herself somewhere without a companion, without parents or a driver or a potential lover—supervisors, all of them: she should be at a point in her life where she is truly learning how to negotiate, how to move, but in this country she does not have the luxury.

"Did you see?" She motions back to Sean, feeling guilty about trying to erase his presence.

"What's that," he says, coming over and squatting next to her.

"Camels—there." Two big dark ones are standing in a sand bowl, and a third trudges its way up one of the dunes.

She doesn't say anything more, just watches them, and he doesn't ruin it for her.

"We camp out here sometimes," he says a minute or two later. "Take bikes up and down, dune buggies."

"Yeah?"

"And there's a shitload of flies."

"I know how to camp," she says. She wants to sound ready to go, in possession of some authority.

Sean grins; he seems amused by this giveaway tone in her voice. "We'll get you out next time then."

"Good." Jill watches all the shapes around her blur into a moonscape; it is a terrain that seems to belong not on this earth or in this time. It has become eerie, starkly comforting. They are marooned. "Thanks for taking me out," she says to Sean. They both squat like that, finding their balance, and let the night wind cool them.

—

Her days are about length. It is now early October, and Jill has been in Saudi Arabia for just over two months. In this time she has shifted and slid, the move halfway around the world upending her whole being. Her former self of school and suburban ease has been reduced to a microscopic thorn, a negligible pain that migrates and twitches sporadically. Back home the class of 1982 has moved on as well. When she was leaving, one of her friends, a girl nearly the valedictorian, confessed to Jill that she really wished not to go straight on to university, that she would rather do nothing at all for a while—for once. This friend is now attending Stanford. Jill is the one who has time, all the time she could have imagined was ever in the world, and nowhere to hang her new self at the end of a day.

Eight miles from the city center and in limbo. Daily exile in a cheaply built prefab housing compound with undesirable companions. One year, she'd promised her father, and during this exchange they'd both pretended to overlook the fact that he didn't have her college tuition. Oh, she thinks, it is special here.

She telephones the administration building for the Army Corps of Engineers, where her father works. "What are the jobs this week," she asks the receptionist, who by now takes her calls in a sympathetic tone, giving out what information she can, which is unfortunately not enough to effect a change in the rhythm of Jill's days.

"Nothing really," she says now. "Unless you've passed the typing test."

"No," Jill says. Her attempt at the typing test was a disaster, a new record of subpar, based on total improvisation of the mechanics. "How about at one of the rec centers?"

"Sorry, dear," the woman says. "Try back next week."

Jill hangs up. It is nine in the morning, and she has now completed the only task that can be deemed an attempt at forward momentum in this life. By half-past seven each workday the compound is empty of men, except for the Yemeni houseboys and the Egyptian racquetball coach. There are so few jobs for women, and those that exist are occupied mainly by the wives. Her mother has one, arranged in advance by her father.

She does not want to be a secretary. She does not wish to serve snacks at a recreation center on one of the U.S. government compounds or tend the game room. For any hope of escape, though, any release from the blankness of her time, this is what she must try for.

Bearing the heat, she dons her Walkman and treks the inside perimeter path of the compound, a half-mile in its entirety. The only creatures are a few wives by the pool, tanning themselves to leather; Jill is from California, but she is still startled by the deep, metallic skin tones these women have achieved. They resemble candied oranges. Later their children will return from the international school to join them or play pinball in the game room. Although Jill has been asked to babysit these children some evenings she is indifferent to them, and feels lobotomized whenever she attempts conversation with the few teenagers her age who exist like lizards, sitting in the sun smoking, or watching videotapes of MTV and *Heavy Metal* recorded by their friends in the States.

She stops at the front gate with its guard post and traffic bar. "Salaam alaykum," she says to the guard, a young Saudi from the National Guard with a machine gun, probably her age. He checks the identity of each returning car in the evening, phones in before allowing guests to proceed. Jill has been told that she may not walk through the gates alone, down the road to the little village, or into the escarpments that jut out above in bleached ochre. What would he do, Jill wonders: shoot her? And who, she thinks, would wish to trespass *in?*

"Alaykum salaam," he replies. This one is cordial; his piety must be compromised, Jill thinks, because of his post here. She, at least, represents a possible compromise, in her shorts and T-shirt, sweaty ponytail swinging; how funny, she thinks, to be a forbidden thing when it has become difficult to sense her own weight or shape.

"And how is your day today?" she asks.

He shrugs, or begins to; it softens into a quiver as he checks himself. "Same-same." The universal reply. At some crossing point between her old world and the Red Sea she'd internalized it, understood it as a stand-in for anything, an opinion or a greeting, unrooted, nearly meaningless.

"It's hot, though," she says.

"All my days the same, miss," he answers, and then shifts his eyes back to the road.

—

In her first weeks she had become friendly with Rowena, a young woman working with a Lebanese architect who did not mind employing her illegally. Jill and Rowena both swam regular laps in the pool—something that, oddly enough, few people seemed to galvanize themselves into doing—and this common ground led to Rowena's including Jill in small evening gatherings at her house. The friendship had been brief; Rowena returned to the States a month later. The coveted job evaporated into the wispy network of favors and connections Jill had not yet penetrated, but Rowena did leave her with a libidinous Arabian housecat as well as a slim entree to her friends Georgia and Caroline. They were sisters, a few years older than Jill. Both had jobs and American boyfriends in their late twenties who were contractors with Saudi firms. Some evenings they invited her along to parties away from the compound and she had met Sean this way, by a pool in a courtyard, one of those nights.

Sean is twenty-four and divorced. This has the tinge of a blunder, to Jill; something embarrassing, on a rung surely lower than the one aimed for.

"When?" she asks him. They are in the souks, looking for a new music store Caroline has told them about that is supposed to be next to an establishment called Perfume Super Europe. The colorful welter of shops and merchandise has so far proved diversionary and misleading. It is evening prayer call, and they are hunched down in a back corridor, eating schwarmas, out of sight of the red-bearded muttawein.

"Put your veil back on," Sean says, picking up the end that is trailing from her shoulder. He can be relaxed and accepting, yet often shifts to unease in public. Earlier he had refused to follow Jill into a lingerie store more splendidly tacky than Frederick's of Holly-wood. The scent of sandalwood bloomed from the doorway to re-veal a combat zone of black-clad women and one hapless Pakistani clerk. The women were ruthless, ordering him up ladders and into bins, yanking lace garter belts and bustiers from packages and fling-ing those deemed unsatisfactory to the floor. The prices, Jill no-ticed, were exorbitant.

The market where Jill and Sean are crouching is both indoors and out; they are lost in a maze of gleaming white-tiled walkways and offshoots. Shop walls and display windows are crammed every which way with goods, and improvised flats of tin or light plank boards act as ceilings. The cover is intermittent; in places the sky is visible and in others, dead-end corridors hold stacks of unused construction material.

"Sweetheart. Veil."

Jill says to him, "I'm trying to eat."

"I don't bloody care. Put it on. It's too close to Ramadan."

"Okay." She complies, first shoveling the rest of the pita in her mouth and wiping the oily sauce from her fingers. The black silk goes back over her hair. "So when?" She looks at him.

He sighs. "Ginger went back to London in March." The look in his eyes is more practical than sad.

"I bet you don't want to talk about this," Jill says. She looks out into the main hallway from her perch on a step. It is mostly quiet, the men having retreated to the interiors, prostrate in worship. The women stand or sit in clusters, waiting. These are the middle-class women, or their maids; the wives of wealthier men sit in the back seats of cars parked in lots or next to the curbs.

"Too right. It's done, and that's all."

"Did she have a job?"

Sean shakes his head, mouth full of food.

"I can understand that, then," she says. "I'm going crazy with-out anything to do all day." They hear the thin whine of a radio, and the store grate next to them rattles up. The scrape echoes re-peatedly as the other shops reopen. Voices start up again, and peo-ple pour into the hall.

"You want to go?" Sean asks. "We'll have a drink back at my place." Jill agrees; she can think of nothing that she wants here, not any object that will divert her enough. They will find their way out now to thrumming Baatha Street, past the store fronts with brightly colored fabric hanging from the ceiling, past the glimmering breast-plates and ropes of gold in 18 or 21 karats, the perfume bottles and the lingerie, the rugs woven in reddish patterns, the coppery pots that throw off the light in luminous glares, out of this cacophonous warren and back into the open sterility of the city where a watch-fulness will hover alongside them, until they are home.

—

A month passes, and then Sean gives Jill something quite valua-ble. They are not in love, Jill thinks; at least she is not, and does not feel such a sentiment from him either. They have fallen into a habit of a kind, easy and unquestioned, and enjoy themselves at the par-ties where it is better to have the cocoon of partnership to retreat to when the expat bullshit factor becomes tedious. If she could define it Jill might say that it is a companionable feeling. Little is expected of her other than sex and the ability to laugh, both of which feel easy to offer up, are in fact a relief. One month is an ad-mirable enough stretch of time, in expatriate Riyadh, for a relation-ship. What Sean gives to her is like a present, maybe a celebration: his houseboy now has a driver's license, and Jill is allowed to call on him for rides.

Sean's house reminds Jill of something in Los Angeles. Low and angled, with large windows and sliding glass doors, hallways and walk-in storage areas to use up space and make the whole ap-pear larger than necessary. A terraced passage, wound over by dried bougainvillea vines and strewn with crunchy petals, stretches from the garage to the front door. There is no grass (the only lawn in Riyadh is a startling expanse in front of the King Faisal Hospital), but instead a patio that wraps around; it holds a blocky swimming pool. Everything is covered in a fine layer of sand, and the leaves of the palm trees droop listlessly over the eight-foot walls surrounding the place.

Sean does not lock the front gate. Jill comes over when she can reach Hassan, the houseboy (*"Allo!"* he barks into the telephone, sounding of pillaged French). This journey from her compound to his house becomes an ordeal of sorts—the telephone lines into the city may be jammed, or Hassan may decline to answer if he is busy or playing backgammon with a neighboring house servant. It is an activity that can command a block of her day and divert her energies. When she is there she does much as she would at home: she swims, she listens to music, and she reads. She has developed an appetite for Robert Ludlum paperbacks, Cold War operative stories stark and mechanical. She pads around the house in a souk dress. She does not bother to mind her wet and sandy footprints when she comes in from the pool; Hassan will sweep up, several times a day.

She is almost like a wife. There most of the day, there when he gets home. She's learned how to mix a tequila sunrise cocktail and vodka martinis by the pitcher. She knows that she is not content, she is in a holding pattern, and she has no idea what to ask for in this place.

Jill makes it a rule that she not help herself to liquor while she is alone; she is not yet that desperate. In any case there is usually company in the evenings. Sean does not distill his own sidiqui grain alcohol but he keeps a good supply, and he has black market connections for supplements of the real stuff. His friends, other men from work, like to avail themselves of his bar. Jill is not much impressed with these friends. They relay tales of their encounters with the ragheads (as they call them), business trivialities stretched to epic proportions with themselves the benevolent victors. Or they speak of other drunken nights, which are in fact most nights. "That Aramco shindig," Michael says. "Yeah, all three girls were ugly," Gregor replies. These two fancy themselves adventuring rogues; Gregor has brought hashish into the country in his boot heel.

"I'm like their fucking babysitter," Sean has told her. "They're attached to me and my bar, like bloody useless limpets." But his choices in this way, like Jill's, are limited.

One of these languid nights, rolled out before them like dough, the talk turns to capital punishment. "You've got to see a beheading," Gregor says to Jill. "Seriously, it's a real rite of passage, your first one."

"There's nothing like that," Michael agrees.

"Well, what is it like?" Jill asks idly. She doesn't believe either of them.

"Oh, come on now," Sean says. He frowns and gets up from the table, shaking the dregs of melted ice and sidiqui in his glass. "Who's for more?"

"I think you should tell her, Sean," Gregor says, tilting back in his chair. When Jill turns to Sean, to hold out her glass, she misunderstands the tightness of his expression. "I'm *fine* to have more," she says, and he takes the glass automatically. Michael and Gregor are both looking straight at him now.

"You cunts," Sean says, just loudly enough. This makes them laugh.

"What—?" Jill turns to them; her face is flushed and she's smiling, looking for the joke. "Right, right," Michael is laughing, and he slaps hands with Gregor.

Sean leans on the bar.

"*Come* on," Jill says. "Tell me a story! I'm bored."

"Fine," Sean says. "I will tell you.

—They're always on Friday mornings," he starts. He looks straight at Gregor. "Early. People start to gather right after sunrise prayer is over. It's actually almost silent the way they come into the clock tower square—they just stream in, sticking together in these little groups, all talking softly. They have the guardsmen out with trucks and guns. You wouldn't believe it," he says. Gregor exchanges a glance with Michael, but both are silent now.

"The men go to one side, the women to the other," Sean says.

"I didn't think the women would be allowed to go," Jill says. She folds her arms over the back of the chair.

"Oh yes," Sean says. He takes a slug of his drink, hands Jill her fresh one. "The women go. This is all part of how it works:

everyone is meant to watch and witness punishment.—Of course, they don't stand together. These things don't start on time, either; the people press in close together, more and more, leaving a space around the chop block and a path to the prison. Finally they bring the prisoner out and walk him up."

"Don't they fight it?" Jill asks. "I just can't imagine that they wouldn't try."

"Well, they're usually drugged. They're bloody well out of it by the time they get up there."

"Really," she says.

"Wouldn't feel much," Michael puts in.

Jill looks at him, scornful. "Well, we don't really *know* that," she says. "That's just one of those things people always say, but we don't really have any idea."

"O.K.—" He tries to wave off her mean mouth.

"They don't seem to really know what's coming," Sean says. "And when it happens at least they have the grace to make it fast. It looks choreographed—like ballet. The executioner swings the sword up high and around. Like taking a golf swing. Then down: one slice. Done."

"*Khalas!*" Michael says, making a cutting motion across his throat, but they ignore him.

"Jesus," Jill says. Then: "Is there a lot of blood?"

Sean nods. "The body sort of jerks back, a reflex. A few big spurts come out of the neck and shoot forward. Once that force is out, then it slumps over. Depending on where the executioner is standing and the force of the blow, he sometimes gets covered in it."

Gregor whistles. "No fuckin' idea, eh Mike," he says.

Jill says to him, "Definitely no fucking idea. Either of you."

"Jilly." Sean is teasing her now. "Come on."

The alcohol hazes through her; she is aware of having something withheld from her, or something twisted. She is not steady. She wants to link her faith somewhere but is suspicious. "You're not lying to me, are you?"

He waits a beat. "No," he replies.

"Then take me," she says. "I want to see it."

"No."

"Why not?"

"Jill. I'm not taking you to bloody Chop-Chop Square, okay?"

Gregor and Michael get up to leave; Jill can tell that they wish no further part of this quarrel in which they have been complicit. After they pass through the living room Sean returns and sits at the table across from her, but he does not meet her gaze.

"Well fuck you too," she says.

———

Late on Thursday afternoon he drives out to the compound. Jill has a washtub of liquor bottles soaking in the back yard, a couple months' worth of empty "tea ration" stock that her father is allowed from the U.S. government. She wears long rubber gloves to scrub the labels from the bottles, working until they dissolve into petaled curls of undecipherable paper, and then she puts the bottles, a few at a time, into a doubled layer of heavy trash bags and smashes them with a hammer. Sean sits in a deck chair, watches her as she keeps methodically at it.

"It's not a bad exchange, I guess," is his offer at conversation. She hauls up a bag, shards poking through in places. The mess goes into a blue trash bin to be wheeled over to the recreation center, where it will join hundreds of other scrubbed and smashed bottles that are disposed of at the dump out near the airport, nicknamed Expat Hill for the swelling, glittering mound of residue that carries the aroma of gin and soap.

"I suppose not," she says after a minute. "My dad gives me the booze, I do the dirty work." Her distracted parents have become liberal in this way, and she squirrels away evidence of her excesses. They must allow her something, here.

"I came to see if you want to drive out to Al-Kharj," he says.

She is still sore at him. This is an offering, however, and she'll take it; she does not know when her next moment will be.

It is clear-skied and around ninety, and the wadi smells fresh as they drive out to the dam. The road narrows as it snakes around and they get farther from the highway. Jill's moodiness lifts as she sees more that is new to her. Stunted mud-walled farm houses are wedged into the spaces between sections of the escarpments, seeming to be extensions of the rocks themselves; palms and scrubby desert bushes are jammed into any available crevice, shading over yards. *Allahu, al' akbar* wavers out from a village mosque, and as they pass by the gates are being closed to the road. Goats wander out, unattended, and chew into the boxes and cans that are stacked ready for disposal.

The dam rises sharply in front of them after they take a long S-curve. The wadi pinches close here, and the thick dam wall spans only a few hundred feet across. Sean pulls off the road. He parks in a small empty lot where a lone Toyota truck sits next to a shed.

"The caretaker's probably praying or sleeping," he observes as he gets out.

Jill is disappointed; this does not seem like very much, this stagnant place. It is still and soundless. The truck's motor, turned off, expels a retch into the air.

Sean is pocketing his keys, walking to the stairs that rise steep to the top of the dam. "Up and over," he says, pointing.

Jill is dubious, but she gathers up her dress, abayah over it, and follows.

The climb is arduous. Somehow, this is funny; Sean has a gain on Jill, and keeps looking back down at her, pretending that he isn't tired. The air has begun to revive her, and the wind blows in her face. They are ascending, she does not know to where, and this act of scaling something is unalloyed. Near the top Sean hops up the steps on his right foot, one at a time, clearly with some effort. When he is on the lip of the wall he looks back and he is red-faced, and his shirt has become damp from sweat. He waves at her.

"All *right*," she calls up to him, laughing. He looks good to her there, out of breath from hopping up like that, grinning like a boy. She takes air into her lungs and stamps up each step to the top, making her calves ache.

He is already going down the other side. "We're here," she hears him say. The little farm is spread out below them, the tilled rows like a flocked cloth. Palms sprout at intervals around the pools of water collected from the irrigation ditch that runs from the dike wall.

"It's lovely!" she says, and her words are tossed back to her from the wadi. She picks her way down the steps and at the bottom the earth smells watered, clumps from residual dampness when she turns her toes into it. A sweetish tang wafts up to her, along with smoke from a smoldering compost heap next to a farmhouse across the field. Squat houses cluster beyond the farm and down a single dirt path where there are no people that Jill can see.

Sean has reached the house and motions for her to stop at the edge of the field. A man comes toward him, followed by two others nearly identical in their white thobes and ghotras. Behind them at the door is a figure garbed in black. Jill can see her face, and realizes that she is young. The girl withdraws and Jill instinctively puts her own veil back over her hair.

"It's fine," Sean says, walking back to where she waits. "He doesn't mind if we sit out under the palms."

The field is small, and Jill cannot tell what might grow here in the sandy dirt. The water comes from an underground river and gurgles up where the palms clump at a corner of the field. The leaves offer a canopy for them, and they sit underneath. Jill chooses a date from a little cloth bundle that the farmer has given to Sean. It is sticky, and juices like a wizened plum.

"It's so peaceful out here," Sean says after a while.

"It is. I love it."

He looks at her, and she cannot decipher it exactly. "What?" she says. He shakes his head then. "Never mind," is his reply. The breeze lightly whistles around them, and the palms sigh in the air.

"So you'll go back, right?" he says abruptly.

"Back?"

"Home. To college."

"Well, yes," she says. "Sure." She feels her impatience flick into a frown, smoothes it. She realizes that she has disengaged from what comes next. Why he would put it to her like this, she does not know; that she would be expected to elucidate is a mystery. She has alighted here, and she will go again. She has not been asked anything, not explicitly, but she feels put upon, and unfairly so.

She decides to exhibit a pique, one that she will play out as humorously petulant. "Oh, you," she says, getting up to stretch. She goes to the palm tree, lightly like a dancer. With her arm outstretched she steadies herself with her fingertips, lifts up in a mock arabesque, imagines him looking, behind her. Her long dress has become transparent in the light and the shape of her raised leg is visible. She puts her other hand on her head and wriggles goofily. About to turn back to him, she is arrested by a glimpse of the girl in black, who has come out of the rear door of the farmhouse and is watching Jill.

"Hey," Jill says. A field separates them, they are not close enough for the girl to hear her, but Jill smiles, hoping that the girl will be able to see that. She evidently does; ducking her head, curiosity gets the better of her and she looks up again. A pigeon scuttles in front of her and the girl, holding Jill's gaze, kicks at it. Now Jill laughs.

"What," Sean says, but Jill shushes him.

The girl's veil has slipped from her head now. Jill can see her eyes lighting out from her dark face. Waving at her, she does a little dance step. The girl has her hands on her veil, about to return it to her head, but first she laughs, wide and open, and Jill is restored, thinking it a lovely moment. Later, she thinks that she must have closed her eyes, causing her to miss the rush of movement before the sound. She hears a sharp bleat, nearly like a goat. The girl is struck in the head, she cowers under a barrage of slaps and chops from one of the men, and then she is shoved and pushed, through the door and back inside, swallowed up.

"No!" Jill yells out, and her cry is loud. "My god!"

"Shhh, Jill, hey now," Sean says. She turns to find him standing behind her; he has seen it all. This churns her helplessness into fury. "How could you—"

"What," he says.

"How could you not do anything!"

34

"It's horrible, I know," he says to her. "I wish I could do something."

Jill feels his hands on her shoulders, and knows that his tone is meant to soothe, although it does not. "It's my fault," she says then. "I shouldn't have looked at her."

"No," Sean says, "it's just the way it is."

She wishes that she could blame him. What she hears in his voice, the flatness and a kind of resignation, or acceptance, is the element that seems to dilute everything, and this she cannot parry.

They walk back to the truck in silence. Sean goes briskly, as if with purpose. Jill climbs the stairs in a slow rhythm. At the top she pauses at a haunting sound in the air that is like a whippoorwill, only there are not whippoorwills anywhere here, where she is so far from anything. The wind has come up and it plays symphonic tricks.

Sean is waiting in the truck; Jill steps in and clicks her door shut. She will take something up tomorrow. If it is time she has been given then there must be something that she can get out of it. Put it on her side, if not defined. She can set herself a schedule.

"There'll be a few people round tonight," Sean says, while Jill is arranging her abayah in her lap. She sees time there in his face. A small piece of it has transpired, accreting with the others that have passed over him.

"I'll go home, I think."

He starts the engine. "Have it your way," he says. They pull onto the road. She hears from him neutrality—not anger, or impatience, nor surprise. It is as if everything will roll out again the next day, she will ask him another question and he will fashion an answer as best he can, as well as he will, and it is her choice to accept it or to decline.

Jill has the feeling of slipping over a ledge, and what falls blossoms into a new, sharp sorrow. It is exhilarating. As they drive down the road the sun is setting beautifully again, tingeing the village and pouring over the walls and roofs and covering anything they have just seen.

She cranks the window down and leans on the ledge, letting the wind slam her and leaving her arm carelessly bare. She waits for Sean to yell at her but he does not. Intuiting then that she should offer him no comfort, she hums to herself as they approach the highway. His presence is now a kind of burden to her, and as long as she is with him she will hold his fears secret and they will be heavier than her own. Already she is restless. She watches him as he drives steadily, in control of the truck. He is staring at the road ahead and taking nothing in; a distant speck becomes another vehicle, and he fixes on it as it approaches in case it is something, anything, interesting.

SLOW STATELY DANCE

IN TRIPLE TIME

Looping the loop, 1946. It was nothing like diving over the chalk cliffs from Folkestone to Dover, where sun dappled the ocean below and sent up a glare that could stun a man into going the wrong direction. He'd managed to be in the thick of it mostly on bright days, only once or twice chasing Messerschmitts in the fog that he'd been told would never let up. As a matter of fact that was simply not true: like other places one is told about. Of the Arabian desert, others like him had certainly come before, but of the words written about it Gus was ignorant. Driving the plane into the sharpest, sheerest blue sky he'd seen since a boy, he saw below what he had not been able to fully imagine when standing in its midst.

There was a name for every ridge, every dune. As Gus caught an updraft, preparing to whip over and down, he could hear Basim shouting from the passenger seat in front of him. The machine was old, a light-model biplane. If there had once been a gun rig there was no longer any trace of it. Falling into the downdraft the two men saw the sands gleaming like waves: they rippled and broke, and Gus could figure, without having to hear Basim's explanations, the patterns made by the shifting winds. It was a map.

Gus took the nose higher for one last flip. Then they looked down at sky, up at land, and after the horizons righted themselves again their goggles continued to defy gravity, remaining on their foreheads. Gus dropped the plane into a lazy spiral, the world from five thousand feet becoming closer and real again, slowly then faster then slower still.

Back on the ground, taxiing short in the tugging sand, the colors and lines of the landscape and the objects there were distinct. There were tents, jeeps, camels, men. That morning Gus had at first failed to discern the plane itself, sitting parked, which like everything else seemed to blend into an endless beige. Now he was blinded as if by a rainbow. When Basim climbed out of his seat and asked him if he'd understood, Gus was startled by the bronze hue of his friend's face. Then he said that he hadn't been able to hear much through the wind. "But you understand," Basim said, clasping him by the shoulders and looking at him carefully. Well yes, Gus said, he did.

———

Basim bin Fadil al-Aban was the son of long traditions and he knew that no man like Gus, no parched-plain roaming Texan boy, would ever read the desert as well as he could himself. And his own skills—though valid—were something he seemed determined to shuck off. This lack of seriousness drove his father to a state of suspended grief. What good was it for Basim to have this bedu knowledge in his blood, if he squandered it on airplanes and automobiles and sporting with hawks? Why these things? It was talent wasted without care.

In Naples Gus had learned these particulars from Basim. They talked about fathers as a way of introduction. Gus had been released from service, he said, and was not inclined to return home. He and his new friend took in the cities of North Africa and the Mediterranean, and for a time the fascination of shoddy cafes and winding alleys was enough. (Remember, his war had been from the air. What he understood was the bird's-eye view: a shoulder of coastline, a grid of city or town shot over.) Grounded now, he had already wandered; with Basim it was no longer desultory. "It's not Texas," Gus said. In return for Basim's stories about the desert he described the dry terrain and ranchlands forty miles south of Abilene. He'd been relieved to get away from that flat, stretched place where the dirt smelled sour and his people let the landscape win. His tales soon ran out; he couldn't compete. Basim wound digressions into his narratives, taking up afternoons while they sat drinking coffee at tables on the streets next to other young men of various background and nationality.

Talk of battles was winding down. There was only so much repetition to be wrung from them. Gus and Basim reached a high pitch in their restlessness, a state that surpassed even that of the others strewn among the conjoining continents in that first year after the war. They were surprised at how quickly people were getting on. There was a drifting back, and then a tightening. *What did you do. Who are you. What do you want.* Where two months earlier they had slipped through with little notice—Basim, after all, might be Indian, with his excellent lilting English—it was clear that despair on a grand scale did not exhaust suspicion.

They continued south.

In Cairo, the effects of unsettling were vibrant. Here were skins of all colors, and different uniforms—many pilfered or inauthentic. The two young men could breathe. Basim knew the city well, having attended its university. They could certainly have gone to the Auberge; Basim had afforded it during his student days and talked of the dancing and the stages and crystal-lit waterfalls and pools. Instead he directed them to a neighborhood where the doorways were low and heavy curtains fell across the archways. He lifted one of these and Gus looked down into a cellar room with a dozen or so small tables crowded together, where men watched a dancer thrash her hips to a drumbeat and cymbals. The lanterns hooked to the wall gave off a sickly light and the girl's eyes glittered like a lizard's. So this is how it's supposed to be, Gus must have thought, and he was depressed. Turning back to the door, he saw that Basim had dropped the curtain and disappeared.

The next day Basim suddenly pitched his coffee out of its cup onto the stone floor of the establishment where they were sitting. "This is swill," he said, loud enough for the barman to hear. "Tastes like goat piss." Gus understood that this unusually rude display meant that it was time they moved on.

From the port at the Red Sea, Basim hired three men to drive them as far as the good roads went, out to the Nejd plateau. From there they would find the family. Two weeks, or a little more—the trip would have taken that long, then. Sleeping in tents when the sun was high, making their way from village to well to date palm grove at night. It was new to Gus, so they did not hurry and stayed in places where Basim's father was known: Fadil bin Saleh al-Aban's son could expect hospitality. Much later, it was suggested that this journey could have been the beginning of something else. At the time it was expected only that Basim was coming home. The two young men paraded themselves into camp in midsummer, each behind the wheel of a jeep; the arrival was viewed with indulgence, to be absorbed seamlessly into the life there that would go on as it had.

—

Aini. Nawar. Huma. Ghusun. Thurayya. *My five beautiful sisters,* Basim said, although this was not strictly the truth. He was proud that they trooped from the dim space of the family mahram, pushing the brightly colored curtains aside to come out of the tent and stand in a line. None could hide their smiles. Thurayya and Ghusun, twelve and thirteen that summer, jumped at Basim and giggled wildly with their heads pushed into his chest.

"You see they are not afraid—but take a good look at them now, before my older brother comes," Basim said to Gus. The two girls fought to get at the pockets of his field jacket. "Almost still children," Basim said.

Gus stood his place in the blowing sand; they had seen no women since leaving the sea. Everyone at the port had been rushing to gather and embark—who knew where to, and he hadn't cared. Now the three eldest sisters pulled into themselves, holding veils across their faces so that only their eyes and the bridges of three similar broad noses were visible. (They had not seen their brother in some years; he must have known that.) The black coverings hid Aini's full plain cheeks, Nawar's jutting incisors, and Huma's graceless jaw, but it was still possible to see the caution that rode their features down like gravity. Yet Basim disengaged himself from the quick dark ones to touch the other three in turn gently, resting his hand on each to kiss them once, twice, each side before holding them off at arm's length. His expression was kind.

The postcards in Basim's pocket were a present for the younger girls. Thurayya was smaller but grabbed faster than her sister Ghusun; she darted away, hair flying, and looked back at Gus once before slipping into the tent.

It must have been more than a year since the family had moved anywhere, Basim explained to Gus. His eyes traveled over the smooth sand, detecting a shallow groove leading away from the encampment where regular footsteps had tamped down the layers. And he claimed to be able to gauge a duration from the degree to which the poles of the tents had settled. His own childhood summers had been spent high in the mountains, in a village carved into the slopes; autumns, when the air was cooler again, they journeyed back near the farm in time to see the date palms hanging with fruit and ready to harvest. He took Gus to the top of the rocky escarpments. The cliffs sheltered the camp from high winds, and green scrubby plants burst from the rocks in a profusion that carried all the way down to the nestled valley of the farm, some two miles away. So much had changed. The edges of the groves touched a village now, and a single road made its way along the plateau, snakelike, until it met the larger road that went all the way to the city.

They had arrived from the other direction. Looking behind him, Gus felt the press of vast nothingness, though he knew he'd come through it to get where he was. The camp below appeared to him in miniature. The escarpments were not very high; nevertheless the arrangement of tents looked like dolls' houses made of cards, the jeeps were small as toys, and the animals no larger than insects.

There were no lines or tracks anymore to evidence the journey they had made. It was as if everything had been dropped from the sky, or sprouted from underneath the sand. Yet there was movement: each thing that stirred made a puff or shadow before settling again. The back flap of the tent flicked out, then down, and then was held out again by an unseen hand.

———

Hah! the two youngest girls said to each other back in the tent, where they fingered the postcards taken from Basim's clothes. Ghusun and Thurayya held each one up to the thin beam of sunlight peeking through the slit where they had untied a hank of goat's wool. The corner was otherwise held fast in darkness by patterned rugs knotted firmly together to poles. They were practiced at needing only this weak bit of light. *Hah hah.* Here, this is Constantinople in the rain; see how the cobbles of the street glimmer with wet. Here's the Parthenon, where Basim sat one day and wrote out a letter they cherished for its intent, though they could read only a handful of the words. This is Cairo. There is the university, they exclaimed, where their brother was until he decided his duty was with the North African troops of the Allies. But now he had come home.

Their mother called from the front room but the girls waited. If they were very quiet, they knew she would think they were out with the lambs—the young animals were theirs still to watch, although one of their father's men came to herd them back to the farm every day. Or she might think they were with their aunts. Thurayya and Ghusun did not want to go to their aunts' tent. They resented their dour moods. The two older women transferred the energy of their personal dissatisfactions and quarrels to the girls, making them sort rice or crank the wheel of the sewing machine while they mended their sons' thobes. The girls did not like their cousins, seven of them, all boys.

Ghusun pulled at the tangles in her hair. Thurayya looked intently again at the postcards: Athens. Tangiers. Rome. These were the words she knew; before Basim went away, he had shown her a book with a map of the world, pointing to where he would go.

It was late in the day and the girls peered out of the tent to watch Basim and their father standing together at the base of the ochre escarpments. The visitor was nowhere to be seen. Their brother had not changed out of his khaki fatigues and to the girls he looked like a visitor too. He spoke animatedly while Fadil bin Saleh al-Aban stood in his long white thobe, holding the sheath of his slaughtering knife. Their fine sharp heads nodded together. Thurayya and Ghusun had inherited the same definitions: high brows and slim, precise noses and lips. Their other siblings had been dealt the coarser features of Fadil's first wife. Now their brother Omar arrived. The girls covered their mouths and laughed at the sight of his fat backside swishing under his dress; his wives had the same pronounced bottom and waddle. The greeting between the brothers was a brief formality of two kisses, and then the three men made quick work of the killing.

They were not squeamish girls. First they saw a lamb, pierced fast in the throat so that it scarcely had time to cry. One of Omar's sons held a pail to catch the blood while Basim slaughtered a fat young goat. The girls were excited to see what came last: a camel calf, one of the softest things from that year's herd. Basim bowed to his father and led the animal to him. Omar, intent now on supervising the remaining butchery of the goat as well as the lamb, did not look up as Basim and Fadil worked together, the older man pulling the reins to the ground while the younger swiftly tied all four legs together with rope. Fadil punctured the camel's heart, then drew the knife through its neck.

It was to be a big feast, Thurayya and Ghusun decided. They wondered if the visitor would eat these offerings. And where was he now? Their mother called again, her voice coming closer to the dividing curtain, and the girls pulled the tent flap back in before she could catch them looking.

———

43

Gus watched Basim's mother hang copper lanterns and silver coin chains in the large front room of the family tent. From a hundred feet away, the ornaments winked in the sun in flashes that seemed to Gus like some kind of desert Morse code.

The front flap of the tent was open to the air. Basim's mother lifted an incense burner, which looked like an ornate spinning top, to a hook in the peak of the ceiling. One of the older sisters—Gus could not tell which—came in to change the front dividing curtain to a sheer panel of embroidered gold. Behind it was another in a deep plummy shade, obscuring the family quarters. In his own tent, the standard Army issue of dun-colored cloth and tarps, Gus unpacked his belongings and arranged cot, folding desk, boots, canteen. He felt effete and ridiculous, like an explorer awaiting the arrival of a cushioned rattan lounge. His movements were routine but awkward. He was a skewed mirror image of the smooth domesticity playing out across the stretch of sand that separated the dwellings.

He should have known that it would be different. His plans remained unformed; flying had gotten him from the despair of a drying-up Texas farm to England and then farther, where he had lingered alone, until Basim. How easy it had been to drift. There were few questions asked, and any asked were glossed over; an American could work as well as anyone else, with so much to fix and rebuild, everywhere. He left town after town pocked with savage destruction—and gradually, he had allowed some grand idea of reparation to fill in the blank grooves of his mind.

"A man without a place," Basim said to him often, in his jovial open manner. It was the big question for young men, a philosophy. Gus had vaulted from one understanding of the world to another. Texas had become impossible and thank god for the war; thank god. Men became different when they were only with other men.

Now Basim offered a recast of their many discussions on this matter. He stretched his arms up and leaned on the front poles of Gus's tent. "So," he said, smiling broadly, "your new place, for now." The fabric of his shirt was stained with sweat and blood from the slaughter and pulled taut against the outline of his ribcage. His scent—the pungency of their three weeks' journey together—hit Gus full-on. He closed his eyes. When he blinked them open, Basim's mother stood at the tent flap next to her son with a tray of dates and flatbread. Basim shouted his approval of this and kissed and hugged her. He hastened to describe to Gus the superior provenance of the dates, his father's plentiful groves and allotments, the delicious bread recipe unsurpassed by any woman in their tribe. His voice was no longer languid, and his mother's gaze moved from her son's laughing face to the tightened features of the boy he had brought home.

———

His name means "smiling," his beloved second son's. The first of course was Omar, and if his naming seems unimaginative it should not be thought so; where many parents chose it from the custom of designating *first son,* it should be known that there was a debt of honor as well, to the memory of the man who had been instrumental in my father's security and wealth. But Omar from the start was hard to love. Was it his shameful punyness, his complaining cries that even his mother could not claim as robust? He did not improve as he grew and later he simply invoked his birthright. It was clear that he would work to earn nothing. Long years followed, where three dull obedient daughters came and father wearied of packing and moving this family with the seasons. He wearied still more when his wife died in the time of the long drought. Guilty over not loving her, he took as his next wife her sister, widowed and presumed barren. Basim, they say, was born in a year when the well in the northern oasis was nearly dry and the camels' humps were sagging with malnourishment. Yet he thrived, and laughed when bounced or tickled, and a swinging pouch was fashioned in which Basim rode on his father's back into the desert. And somehow this general good nature was carried on with the next two girls. If Basim was the favorite, we did not suffer for it and had more regard from our father than did our elders. Our smiling brother. Even now it is difficult to think of him as *was,* somebody gone, someone I once understood so well.

———

Omar, watching in the firelight, watching his father, seeing how he kneels down close, leg to leg when he speaks in Basim's ear. Basim with his arm tossed over his friend's shoulder, making everyone laugh, the neighboring men who had come calling out their names, names of things they pointed to, making Gus repeat after them. Now Basim turning the game to instruct again, in that language where the words sounded slurry and unfinished. The visitor bestowed with a checkered ghotra and band for his head, wrapping it on expertly—too expertly—for roars of approval. The night was wearing on and the platters of meat and rice had been passed in to the women, the sisters and mothers, virgin and married, waiting behind the curtains stretching, dozing, nursing, the things they did there out of view.

Sitting cross-legged between the two curtains, the two youngest sisters, in that small dim space, skin prickled all over. *Airplane,* they whispered to each other, *Ab-ih-lene. Abilene.* Fadil bin Saleh al-Aban roasted coffee beans for his guests, jumped up to clap four times, gestured for Basim to lead a sword dance while the beans were pounded and boiled. The smell of cumin wafted through the tent and the girls tapped their fingers on their thighs in time with the drumbeats. Thurayya, draped in a rough cotton gown the color of pomegranates, eyes missing nothing, catching the dark look from Omar as her slight movements caused the curtain to stir, and holding that look, then going past him, to the restored authority of father and best-loved son.

———

Well, Nida. She never came while the visitor was there; of course she would not. The agreement between Fadil bin Saleh al-Aban and Nida's father was long-standing, as those arrangements were. And Fadil's position afforded him the luxury of bargaining well: he had what he needed, money earned from service to the House of Saud, control over a large swathe of land, and the betrothals of his children could raise the standing of other families. Years earlier there had been the necessity of bridges between lesser or volatile tribesmen. Omar's two wives were no great beauties but—it was said—how cannily accurate the unions had turned out to be! Less hidden laughter attached to the fate of the first three daughters, poor things. A husband, a child dead; well, a father like that need hardly pair them again, if he could keep them. Nida's father knew what he possessed: a flock of young females striking in looks and serene of temperament, with Nida the loveliest of all. This next bridge with Basim would have life the others had not.

But who carried the higher value now—a son with experience in the world, or the daughter grown into beauty so legendary that in the desert, our world, the legend seemed to fill it? These matters required decorum. The negotiations of pride would be sorted through by the fathers.

The timing was not right. This was sensed by everyone.

And there was Aini. That summer she had taken her place again with her sisters, and the woman who was not her mother, in the home she remembered from an earlier time. She was the first daughter. She moved with care: an old metal bin on her shoulder, a brush switched across the rug to scatter sand. Ordering, making tidy. There was little for her to do. Even Nawar and Huma had not suffered such a disgrace as she. Her husband was still living, but he had banished her—she brought death, he said, their children one by one and others in his village as well, though he was kept whole and alive to bear witness. It was said he was mad, to claim he knew what was willed. But still people wondered. Had Basim not come home, they might not have forgotten.

No, Nida was never there. She never did come, and Basim did not speak of her, and as the days went by time remained suspended like a bundle that should be let down but was not. Our brother was home. But behind his smiles it was as if he were examining objects from another life, and his face said that he would never go to her.

———

Gus did not write letters to anyone. He woke early from instinct; as a boy he'd always liked to see the sun rise. Later this habit served him well, and he had no trouble shaking off sleep to get into the fields of the farm and then again in England, where he woke refreshed to the dawn after night bombing raids and mere hours of rest. Here in the desert he opened his eyes to discover the sun burning up the horizon as the moon fell down over his shoulder. Gus sat and watched with his folding desk on his lap. He felt that he should be writing it down, but for whom? The paper in the box had hardly been depleted since he'd left Texas—fingering it, Gus could not recall how many years had gone by since he'd written a word to his family but he did know that the paper had come in handy for rolling cigarettes.

One thing he discovered too was that there was often not much need of talking. Most days he followed along with Basim as his friend toured the lands with his father. Fadil bin Saleh al-Aban had much to show his son: the improved irrigation was making the farm and date groves lush and the animals fat. He joked that this settling was what came with old age. Some of the Arabic registered with Gus—he was recording it absently, he realized—but outside of the boisterous evening gatherings, little was expected from him. He was growing into the terrain. During these expeditions with Basim and his father one of them would occasionally say something to him, all smiles, and he would respond, punctuating the conversation with a pitch that echoed in a different key. The three men rode quietly on horseback and Fadil sometimes drew close to his son, looking out across the plateau as he spoke. Gus waited behind them.

Yes, he should have known it would be different here.

———

48

The summer's heat reached its apex. Then it dropped off one day, bringing up a wind that blew in remnants of plant life along with a whipping tail of red sand. The women in the camp rushed about tying down the knots of the tents, frantically beating back the sand that was forced through with the sharp gusts. Spouts rose up from the ground and spat grains in circles. It made a mess of things, but the cool was worth the nuisance. To the youngest girls it was a game. "*Shamal, shamal!*" they cried, laughing, as they ran around outside the tent. Thurayya twirled, letting the wind make a balloon of her dress.

"No, habib," Basim told her. "It will not be a big storm." He explained to Gus that the weather was performing its customary tease for this time of year: it would soon be hot again, but not quite so much. The winds were a signal that the season was preparing a change.

When the winds settled again a new energy remained in the camp. Now there was anticipation. Each day Basim and his father assessed the date palms, testing for ripeness. It was a matter for precise calculation. Fadil was proud that his son remembered: Basim split each fruit carefully, touching his tongue to seed, running a finger over the shining skin.

There were other changes, things that the family had not seen before. One morning Basim and Gus rode away early in one of the jeeps, driving it up the steep road into the escarpments and onto the ridge, taking the fork to the large paved road to Riyadh. The city was only a half-day's drive. Most in the camp and the village had never been there. Thurayya and Ghusun climbed the rocky path to wave at their brother as he sped away; he had told them he would come back with a surprise.

When the sisters saw his jeep returning they jumped up in excitement. They ran across the sand to meet him and then they stopped: their brother was alone.

And then they heard it, first a buzzing, then a roar, and everyone in the camp came running now, exclaiming in alarm and then wonder as the loudness increased overhead and an arm of shadow seemed to eclipse the sun. They looked up and the thing rushed over them, gliding down and down and down. As it went past Thurayya knew at once that it was no bird, and she saw a man sitting inside it, and he waved, and her brother returned the gesture and came over to pick her up on his shoulder so that she could see the final swoop as the thing slid smoothly from sky to earth some distance away. It came to a stop and sand billowed around it in a cloud.

"That is an *airplane*," Basim said to Thurayya, and she remembered the word. Clapping and cheering now with her brother, while her older sisters shook their heads and returned to the safety of the tent, she loved this new thing that she saw.

———

Athens. Tangiers. Constantinople in the rain. We had known these things in our hearts, and now we could fashion them: Basim told us stories, and he helped us to trace the words on the cards with our fingers, and then with a pen on the visitor's clean sheets of paper, which we held up to the light when they were covered with our markings and seemed to tell two tales, one on each side. We folded the papers around each picture to keep the new stories together. Our brother showed us books he had tied up with a strap: most were senseless to us, the words unknowable in stark tiny print. One was smaller than the others, with fewer pages. It showed the letters one by one, curling, and we wondered at how a hand had drawn them there so that they did not smear when we touched them.

Every evening, while the visitor stayed on, Basim gathered the men from the camps and the village. They laughed and talked together and we watched from behind the curtain. Each night brought something else new. One time it was a wooden box that opened up to display a horn. The visitor fixed a flat disc to the top of the box and Basim showed how to turn a handle on the side, and when this happened the horn made strange scratching sounds and piped out a song that screeched and bounced. The same song was repeated when the handle was turned again. This time we learned from the visitor *Virginia*, and *reel*—it was a dance, he said, for men

50

and women, but here, in the desert, we watched the men together, making lines that formed and broke and came together again.

Now when our aunts called for us we refused to hear them. Aini could go, and we scuttled away. When our cousins came too close from their tent we ignored them; when Omar glared at our books we turned our backs, knowing he dared to say nothing. There was Basim, in sun or in firelight. The visitor was always close by. Perhaps we should have known that there would come a point soon when all that we saw must be taken away again, but we did not, and we continued to watch and grow bold.

———

The other things they saw: that a jeep taken up the low bowl of a dune could skim without sinking, then seem to almost plummet as it was whirled back around. If it tipped too far, bars overhead made it roll and you were not hurt so long as you were buckled in and held onto your seat. The sand was soft. Once at dusk, in the lull between first evening prayer and the meal, Basim drove while Ghusun and Thurayya scrambled around in the backseat, chattering and pointing at the roadside tea shacks they had seen before only from the distance of their seasonal caravan.

"Careful," Gus said to them from the front, when a bump knocked Ghusun back into her seat. It was the only thing he said to them. The girls quieted to watch a man coaxing a camel into the back of a truck bed. Two black-clad women were sitting there already, one on each tire rise. The camel settled between them and the man hopped into the driver's seat, gunned the engine and tore off in a cloud of sand.

And they saw that a small plane could make loops in the sky. The sisters climbed the escarpments and shielded their eyes against the hot sun, looking straight ahead for miles and miles north, as Basim had told them to. Aini and Huma and Nawar stood still and seemed to be thinking of nothing. After a short while they called to their younger sisters to return home. Thurayya and Ghusun refused: they wanted to stay and watch the distant toy-like machine, jerking around in the sky as if on strings. Nawar hesitated, hovering for a moment as if attached by a string herself to the retreating backs of the two eldest who were picking their way back down the slope. *Yellah*, she said softly, you must hurry before Omar comes.

Dusty and happily tired, dresses torn from where sharp rocks and brush had snagged them, the two girls wandered back late together. Hand in hand, they came from the path to find Omar waiting for them by the camel hitch. "Lazy, disobedient things!" he shouted. "Little animals. I know where you've been." He raised a hand to strike them.

"Yes—you do it," Thurayya said, crossing her arms over her chest. He hit her and she stood where she was. Ghusun stepped out of reach but Thurayya stared at her brother levelly, the mark from his hand on her cheek. She lifted her chin, then spat on the ground. "*That* is what I think," she said. "Don't touch me again. I'll tell father." She pulled Ghusun by the wrist and back along the path to camp. The umber rays of the sunset reddened Omar's face even more than it already was, and Thurayya gloated over her shoulder at the sight as she stalked away.

At the camp that night Omar sat alone in shadow. Between the curtains Thurayya simmered with a new rush of feeling, her face bare and thrust forward still, as if the print from his hand were indelible.

Later, that night when so many stars pierced the black, the girls were discovered rolled in a blanket and sleeping outside the back flap of the men's majlis. Yanked awake by Omar, they did not know where to look as the three men of their family paced off and shouted. They had not only been watching, but dancing—for proof Omar gestured at the tracks their feet had left in the damp sand, in the pattern of the square dance the visitor had been demonstrating to the men inside. It had been weeks of this, Omar said, and now it was enough. The elder sisters were already source for ridicule but should these youngest become so too? They were being corrupted, the family embarrassed. "My brother must do *his* duty now," he said. Fadil bin Saleh al-Aban, though loving the other better, at last agreed with his first son.

Basim's face—that smiling brother—was like a stone, unreadable though it may want to weep from within.

—

Thurayya, kicking idly at her sleeping sister's feet, rolling over on her stomach to inch up to the corner of the tent. Hearing voices float and waver, grow urgent. The bindings untied from the pole with her sure fingers now, knowing that she needed to hurry, hurry. Looking out through the crack and there were the two figures standing together by the visitor's tent, arms clasped and there they held, close, outlined by the light of the lantern from within. They broke apart and the glow went out.

Then she was breathing quietly but hard, fast awake and keen. Tying back the knots to make blackness again and raising herself to a squat with her outlines blending into air. Without waking Ghusun, Thurayya reached her hands up to the little bag hanging from a loop over them and not needing to see, removed the picture postcards and the small cloth-bound alphabet book and the other scrawled-upon papers they had been accumulating like candy treats. Silently digging in the corner where the pole went deep into sand, under the mats, for what seemed like hours until the things could be stowed there and the surface brushed over without a trace. After unwanted sleep Ghusun shaking her hard, leading her outside where the earth stretched away and the visitor's tent was gone, stakes pulled, and the tracks from their brother's jeep left a faint and fading scar.

—

If it was then that the general knowledge began to spread, like anything dark, it was as this: in one way like an understanding anywhere, in any time. Sometimes it was discussed with troubled headshakes and somber tones by the men resting under the date palms. And by the women, the sisters banding tighter in resolution, muting their sadness whenever their mother appeared. She refused any mention of disaster. The three eldest, squeezing mounds of filtered camel's milk into gluey bricks to dry in the sun, were caught by her one morning and struck dumb by the fierce expression on her face. "*Khalas*," she told them, shaming their tongues into submission. From then on Aini and Huma and Nawar telegraphed their thoughts on the matter to one another with their eyes. But Ghusun and Thurayya found more time to walk farther from the camp than they had before. They became expert at tending the young wheat stalks on the farm, nurturing the thyme and rosemary growing between the rows with hands more sensitive than their father's workers. They brought the goats to calve and Thurayya, who had always been so impatient, spent hours supervising the weakest of them. That his youngest daughters were exhibiting industriousness of any kind was a welcome relief to Fadil bin Saleh al-Aban; to forget the disappearance of his son he redoubled his old chieftain's habits, riding away regularly to enforce his benign control over Omar's growing concerns and those of his closest neighbors, and exhausted by these efforts he failed to notice, upon his returns to the home camp, that the knowledge had seeped and hardened into deep divisions within his family.

The burnished autumn season had begun, the air heavy with the sweet smell of ripened dates. Fadil's men took them down from the palms in fat bushels. They loaded them into the remaining jeep to take them to the city markets. Fadil now increasingly allowed for Omar's demands. Ayawah, he would say. Yes, you do it, you do as you like. The youngest sisters were directed to remain at the camp. Under this silent and tense supervision, they did not dare to show any more interest in what lay beyond the confines of their settlement.

The visitor's tent folded down to vanish in the night. Thurayya had missed that moment, even if what she did see, her brother and his friend together, made her know it would happen. For as long as she could believe it she thought he would return. When the jeep was driven back from the markets in the evenings she watched from her corner of the tent; it seemed to her piloted by ghosts. The plane stood waiting, sheltered by the rise of the escarpments. Then one day she watched the men harness it to a team of camels and pull it away.

So now she had all of the questions, the things she did not understand and wanted to know, and there was nobody but Ghusun, who became docile and eager to please. *La,* she said, shaking her head, if Thurayya noticed that Omar was gone and implored her to steal away. The three elder sisters pampered Ghusun and wound her in new veils. They brushed the tangles from her hair, hennaed her wrists; they scrubbed her face clean. They displayed Ghusun to her father when he came home tired, and this daughter seemed to him a relief. Thirteen was not too young for her to be married. Ghusun bound up her breasts with a long cloth, winding and unwinding until she needed no light to do it, releasing herself only to sleep; her sleep was now to Thurayya impenetrable and secret. Though the nights now came in the two stages for that time of year, the soft balm of dusk followed by a sharper cool and deeper sky, Thurayya kept her corner of the tent warmed with the heat of her fury.

And as if in silent unison with her sister, her own body raced to betray her. In her anger she bound herself too, hiding what might otherwise begin to swell, and she willed herself to contract from the inside and felt triumph when she remained dry. Ghusun's bloodflow seemed saturation enough for them both.

"He is young, Thurayya, at least he is that." Ghusun said this on the morning before the wedding. The girls stood together by the pen that had been constructed for the viewing of the dowry animals. It was empty now. Braided tassels around the posts flew up with the breeze. Tomorrow the pen would be full, camels and goats and sheep altogether, prancing skittishly in their confinement.

"Yes," Thurayya said finally. The word came slowly from her tongue.

Ghusun walked away, leaving Thurayya alone in the slanting light. The sun moved over her as she stood there. She remained for some time until clouds gnarled together above; she wondered if there would be rain. There was not, though she continued to watch the sky. When she returned to the tent it was empty. Ghusun's bundles were wrapped up in rugs and placed in a careful row against one curtain. Thurayya watched these too, staring hard as shadow slid its way around her while she sat. Then she must have fallen into sleep, or at least that is how she remembered it, for she knew that one moment she had been watching and gathering the fading light, as if to hold the last of that day, and then it was dark and Ghusun appeared there suddenly and she did not seem real. She held a lantern in her hand and walked slowly to the corner of the tent, looking around her as if finding a place in her mind to record every crevice she had known there and every thing she had shared with her sister, or ever fought over or contested in their girls' life. That choice space by the vent they had fashioned, there: she had conceded it to the younger, who was stronger willed than she. Ghusun moved forward with the lantern and stood on the roll of her bedding. She curved her lips into a smile her sister had not seen before. Thurayya took the lantern and gazed now, transfixed, at the sight of Ghusun made clean and perfumed, bathed, covered only in a robe of golden cotton that was sheer enough to show the form of her body beneath. Her sister seemed to shimmer there, as if she were preparing to disappear. Then her lines became clear again. Before Thurayya's eyes her shape adapted rapidly and she saw it all: not only her wedding night, but her children and her happiness and her unhappiness, too, everything etched around her, all the coming years. *I am ready,* Ghusun said.

And that next day at the wedding, Ghusun was transformed again. It is really true, Thurayya thought; she is leaving. In the tent her sister sat now with her new husband and was viewed by all. She was in bridal finery, draped ear to ear with veils and coins. Her eyes, rimmed in kohl, peered out and only once—with one look— were they the eyes Thurayya could say she knew. The guests paid respects and their father accepted congratulations, together with Omar, for a match well made. There was feasting and laughter and the noise went on into the night. They were celebrating a child's leaving and through it they were forgetting another's. The sounds of the drums were joyous and that joy was what was there on the faces, hiding truths. The night would erase. Thurayya's anger remained her own. And after that night the knowledge now unspoken —as if Omar had ever been the only son—would stay buried in the set lines of Fadil bin Saleh al-Aban's face and behind the darkened corner of the mahram, where sometimes a mother sat looking intently into the distance as if hearing a far-off signal. And the furious youngest, she imagined this:

Over the night the sand stretching out like a sea. Blue light illuminating small dervishes. The eddies and whirls puffed and settled gently, but someone looking with eyes intent and clear would have noted not a speck, not a reach of brush or rock or other life disturbing the surface that poured toward them steadily in the dark. The far dune's edge peaked and shining like a sword in the sky. A sharp cool scent from this edge that was the lie that covered its power: wait, it sang; stay, rest. The swelling and lifting, what must have drowned them in their tent at night, two men alone and heedless of consequences.

THE GRAND TOUR

After a life of living in the desert, Hamid decided to admit a kind of defeat. He was an old man past sixty. By the time he rode into the village of Al-Kharj with his wife, Rafa, and the Texan, Gus, they possessed only the things they tied to the three aging camels and a pair of spindly, recalcitrant mares. Gus asked where they were going, in the mild way Hamid had become accustomed to. "A relation," Hamid told him. "His father owed mine a debt." Gus understood about extended Bedouin families; this relation, then, would take them in.

He had been with the husband and wife—who were childless —since the day nearly twenty-five years earlier when they had rescued him from the aftermath of a storm. He had never meant to survive it. His companion had not. Hamid and Rafa seemed to understand Gus's guilt, and had delivered him up from the wild sands, burying the other and with it, the Texan's past. He was theirs and stayed theirs, through everything. Now Rafa pulled her camel's reins taut and sat high in her seat. She surveyed the last downward slope to the village and said, very softly, "Here we will make another home." Hamid grunted in reply.

Rafa was some years younger than her husband, as was Gus. The Texan had grown into himself (he had been stripped back by his convalescence, Rafa remembered, in both body and mind), and though he remained slight, and the folds of his robes seemed always to find his bones to cling against, the fragility of his appearance was deceptive. His footing in sand was sure, and he was a steady shot with a rifle. On this journey he had been the one to keep them going with kills of small game: they took what they came across, birds and the occasional hare, once a spiny dubh lizard—a delicacy and, especially now, a good omen. That meal had been the day before reaching Al-Kharj; Rafa agreed with her husband that it was indeed good luck, and Gus's providing it seemed to refresh a sense of good will among the three, but as Hamid continued to extol their fortune in the small fire's light Rafa closed her ears to the sound of his voice.

Hamid wanted her appreciation now, as the houses of the village came into sharper view, but what she had said did not achieve its mark.

They turned the camels into the slope for the descent. Hamid was leading them and his camel—the one of worst temper, which gave the beast a semblance of spirit, from a distance at least—traversed the dune in a sloppy diagonal. Behind him Rafa pulled her reins up again, so as not to overtake him. Gus, as always, seemed in no hurry; he lingered on the rise and looped the mares' ropes over his forearm. They would have to be dragged. It was late morning, the sun yet benevolent, and as they got closer to the village the thrum of harvest sounds shimmered up to them. They heard the knock of long knives, the slish and saw as workers carved off the stalks from the palms. The air carried the tang of ripe dates and would, in the weeks ahead, begin to feel weighted with it. Autumn was the perfect time to arrive (as Hamid had said); it was *necessary* they be there. In this way he had flipped their predicament, explaining to Gus and Rafa that his relation would surely require extra hands—so they would offer theirs. How many harvests had he supervised, anyway, in his time? His listeners had remained patient, hearing this throughout the yawning days of their journey; each could tote up, silently, the many oases they had hovered around or circled back to, year in and out, so many years, the others of their tribe falling away from them, dying off (the old women) or knowing better (everyone else). Gus had stayed, and Rafa of course had no choice. She thought: how do we appear now—as sad opportunists? They rode their camels down. The mares brayed in protest, digging in their hooves. The dune melted into the plateau, and Hamid cantered ahead toward the large house ringed with the greenest palms, the most luxurious shade. It was just like him. Sometimes, when his hopes were this high, Rafa overcompensated with a serenity she was afraid did not hide her pity.

She need not have worried so much about how they would be perceived. As they waited a discreet distance away, while Hamid dismounted and went into the house, she admitted to herself that her husband still possessed one reliable talent: for talk. If she and Gus had sometimes endured it with exasperation in the desert (though with Gus, it was difficult to tell), here Hamid's charm rose again just when it needed to. Rafa allowed her camel to amble over to the watering trough at the gate, after a permissive nod from a houseboy who rounded the corner holding a bright green plastic broom. Gus, who had dismounted too and stood with his back turned away, rubbing the flanks of both mares one at a time, to soothe them, was not yet visible. From inside the house Hamid's most jovial voice could be heard, exclaiming in garbled unison with that of his long-lost relation. (A cousin? Rafa could not remember.) But clearly it was not to matter; Hamid had got it right this time. Rafa and Gus were quite a while in the rising heat of midday before Hamid emerged from the house with this other man, who was close in age but with a sheen of prosperity that rounded him out. His torso strained against the belt of his clean tunic; he'd worked many a day of his life, his musculature conveyed, but did not need to now. The two men had had tea and the scent of hot sugar trailed them out of the house. "God willing you have come, as if I had wished for it!" the man said heartily. To Rafa he nodded once, though he did not let his look stay on her; he took only this small liberty, as host, but would not abuse it. He appraised Gus and said, "Good morning," but betrayed no surprise when Gus replied, "Alaykum salaam."

Later, when the afternoon heat softened, Hamid walked around the garden with his host. Bougainvillea vines draped the walls, and young palms sprouted from fresh dirt, their fronds tickling the side of the house. Water burbled in a small concrete pool where pale orange carp glistened below the surface. It was all brand-new, the man said—"just this year, I decided. And why not? I've lived behind the village walls all these years, and it is too crowded. The dates are mine, and I'd rather live among them." He laughed. He was still getting used to the house: it was modern, not like any house Hamid had ever seen, with square rooms set in rows along hallways that pressed in, and blank white walls and spongy carpeting that was white too, and covered every inch of floor, even in the space where Hamid's friend said he was installing a toilet and bathtub. That room was unfinished; the contractors who were proficient with indoor plumbing were all busy in Riyadh and could not spare the time to come to Al-Kharj. "Ah, well," the friend said. "*Inshallah.*" Then he asked Hamid, "Have you seen one?" and described how the toilet would flush.

Hamid must have been shaking his head in fatigue, and the other man took his hand and sat down with him on a bench. "Let's rest," he said, and laughed again easily, for both of them. "We're old men."

"I am grateful," Hamid said after a minute. He needed to say it simply, at least once.

His relative murmured that he too was grateful, and they made the customary back-and-forth of this. It was always a careful dance of words, among men. The debt to Hamid's father would of course be carried through; it was nothing, it was honor, it was nothing. They sat there and Hamid felt a light caress of wind and he closed his eyes for a moment—very briefly. The relative thought, in that instant, *God, don't let him die on me, this unlucky man,* and felt both guilty and righteous for thinking it. Then he decided that if this was what he was burdened with he could at least issue a little test, to see about the state of Hamid's faculties. Guests, after all, had an obligation to entertain, whatever their circumstances. Gossip was always a good tradition. So he asked Hamid about the white man, and Hamid, understanding, began to talk, heightening and coloring his tale as he went along.

—

The village was crowded, but with the exception of the host's new house the buildings in Al-Kharj strained to stand up to tradition. It wasn't easy work; tradition was becoming malleable. "But it's nothing like Riyadh," his host said, referring to the capital city some thirty miles distant. "There—well, soon there won't be anything old left anymore. Nothing." To Hamid the idea of the large city was incomprehensible. He remembered Al-Kharj from so many years before—*how* many, he sometimes asked himself; he'd been young—and what he brought to mind was an image of small but airy mud-walled dwellings, set in lazy semicircles around the mosque that had commanded the center. The mosque had been the highest point, too, and the tower had been simple and washed over with an ochre tint that lent it a sturdy tone. It had been his father who had taken him there, and both had entered for prayers—the only time they had faced Mecca under cover from the sky. The village had been contained and peaceful. Now Hamid looked for this center again, but it did not match his memory. The tower was the same and there remained the respectful space around it, but its solemnity was lessened by the crush of vendor stalls facing it, wares burgeoning from behind counters and around doors. More houses pushed up, over, and between any space in the confused warren of streets. Hamid found he could not walk the streets in a straight line; he had to circumvent jutting corners where rooms had been added on or duck under balconies dripping with wet clothes; vines trailed over walls and dropped dried leaves into the gutters; bicycles were

62

propped in the alleys and children's shrieking laughter bounced and echoed, and seemed as physical as the objects he stepped around.

So: life goes on, Hamid told himself. Of course there is change. At first he did not understand how these people lived like this, with no space between themselves and their neighbors, no method of traveling anywhere of distance and no desire to do it. He and Rafa took up residence with their host, who had, even with his children and their families living there, enough room for them. Putting his unease with modern village life aside, Hamid supervised his friend's date harvest and was glad of the task. It was a good year, and their welcome was extended. Rafa, relegated to a boxy room in the women's corridor of the house, saw her husband less often. She tried to tend to their belongings—though they did not need the same things, and now required others. She had garments untouched by desert dust to wear in the sitting room; these were presented to her by Hamid, covering his embarrassment with bluster, though Rafa detected them as castoffs from their stretched seams and pinprick holes—the host's wife engaged in a careless subterfuge, enough to remind them of their station. What to do with the rugs, the pillows, the battered pots Rafa had set over fires and rinsed clean with sand? The host had two young wives in addition to his first, a large and imperious woman who had been raised in a tent herself, she said. She claimed Rafa's attentions and used her as a way to increase her petty biddings to the younger women. "Country whores," she said of them to Rafa, after sending one scurrying away to fetch them tea. Her tone was affable. "And two is better: so my husband's attentions will not hang one way or the other for long. *Here*—" she called to the youngest wife, the least attractive, dimpled unbecomingly about her jawline. "You go make tea with this, like a real bedu wife." She handed over one of Rafa's copper tureens, which had never been used for this purpose. Rafa said nothing. The girl looked at the pot dubiously, sucking on her upper lip. The first wife laughed—there was no need for even more tea than they'd had—and then dismissed her with a flick of the hand. Rafa never saw the tureen again. Like the other things from their former life, it just vanished.

She would wonder later why she had been so negligent, why she had not gathered their belongings—*her* belongings—in safety. She would think of how little they were worth, and how much.

Gossip was currency with the wife as it was with the host, and Rafa found herself having to perform. At first, naturally, the topic was the Texan—but Rafa felt a mantle of sadness now when she saw Gus, always from a distance, working the fields or tending the animals. To avoid the quandary of where to lodge him, he had, that very first day, pitched his tent at the fringes of the farm. He was mostly solitary and always busy, and in contrast Rafa's indolence felt acute. She had never pitied him before—at least not since his long-ago rescue and recovery—and she felt for him what she might have felt for a weak child, if she had had one. But he was not a child, as the imperious wife pointed out—one day when Rafa, attempting to exhaust the subject, must have overventured her sentiments. She had not been very forthcoming; she knew the wife interrogated her husband at night, in a raspy whisper that came insistently through any wall. *Who is he, is he a simpleton,* and, when the answer didn't satisfy and she proceeded with her own interpretation, Rafa heard the word *disgrace.* Nothing about her, though she was sure her barrenness was fodder for another discussion, carried out more discreetly but with the precisely aimed venom particular to women. It was another thing she would wonder about years later: her naïveté. She had always known that she and Hamid were marked, with the Texan. There had always been questions. They had grown so accustomed to the inquiries—and Hamid's charm had worked for so long—that what she told herself was that she'd simply forgotten how a house of women could boil over. *Nest of vipers,* she would remember. *I should have known.*

———

They stayed in Al-Kharj for three years. Each harvest was better than the last. Hamid's host grew expansive; he was happy to discover that his old relation could provide him with easy company, someone whose indebtedness rendered him agreeable but who could also embellish a tale, insinuate with a flourish. *He speaks no English, though it's his native tongue,* Hamid told him; *he sings, though, or rather hums —they're odd melodies, ones from dances,* he said. "Is he—?" His host turned his hand back and forth. "You know—that way. Something wrong."

"Oh, no," Hamid said. He did not say that Gus had been curled with his back to another man, a bedu, when they found him. Even acquiescence to his host's demands for this running joke could not force that revelation, which he himself did not understand.

"*Malish,*" the host replied, losing interest. He clapped a hand on Hamid's shoulder and steered him to the dim little tea house they went to when they needed respite from the farm and the women.

Rafa was by now shrewd to the maneuverings of the host's first wife, who was secure in her reign over the younger wives and the daughters-in-law of the household. And the role Rafa had assumed for herself was one of a kindly aunt. She cared for the children when their mothers grew bored of them; she soothed when the young wives complained, or a daughter-in-law with low standing wept in frustration, and she never revealed what she heard. But despite her knowledge, she was unprepared for the fury that erupted over the host's eldest daughter when she came of age.

She was a pretty enough girl—though coarsely featured, Rafa thought; the liveliness in her eyes would go hawkish when her figure filled out in the way of her mother's. Her father doted on her, so far as it went—when the girl, in her spoiled impertinence, refused to veil he overrode his wife to insist. Then a visiting uncle saw the girl, one brilliant summer day in the garden, laughing and twirling, whisking her black coverings from her face and then back. The sun's light made her abayah translucent. Enraged by this impropriety— surely the girl was performing for someone, the uncle insisted— anger dissolved the smoothness from Hamid's friend's face and his more vengeful nomad mien was revealed. He beat the girl and demanded to know who had seen her. *No one, it was no one and she was alone*—this was the truth, as her mother knew it, but the woman saw that her husband would not be appeased without a sacrifice, and so she offered up Hamid.

The host's face went black. *Vipers*, Rafa thought sadly from the garden where she had gone to get away from the brunt of the argument, though she heard it all. She leaned into the embrace of the bench and looked the greenery over carefully; she had grown fond of the shade, and the palms and vines had matured nicely in three years' time, and now she knew it as yet one more temporary oasis that she would leave behind.

The shouting continued. Rafa listened to their host's tones of disbelief, the wife's urgent pleas. She listened to the battle crescendo again when Hamid arrived some time later, walking unknowingly into a tempest. Oh, he was innocent: Rafa knew this. She blamed him anyway. She sat there as the voices rose and fell, as the girl wept copiously in her room. *Country whores*, Rafa thought, with no remorse. She imagined, as the shadows turned and she kept to her place, and the wailing stopped, that she heard the girl's crafty breathing through the walls. Sacrifice. It would have to be done. Later when the decision had been made and it was she who took charge of the packing, she looked at the row of closed wooden doors in the women's hall and knew that she could retrieve nothing that had been hers—not that she expected to find her copper pot or the bolster pillow she'd embroidered as a young bride, or anything else that had disappeared during their time there. No, they would have to go with what they could gather. In the morning she had to shake Hamid and remind him of what had happened. He was unbelieving, and maintained this mood in the cantankerous manner of old men who assume that feuds between blood relations are only temporary.

Their host, wishing to contain the bad rumors as long as possible, had arranged for a worker to drive them into the city in a truck normally used to haul produce (the camels and the mares were long dead), and Rafa threw their bundles into the rickety metal bed. She climbed in with them; Hamid took the front seat, and his departing wave to his friend was almost celebratory. Rafa averted her gaze, but not before she caught the host's look sliding back towards his house, to the walls of the village, reassuming his position and shedding her husband and herself and the odd, silent Texan as merely a minor interruption in his life. The driver gunned the engine and backed up as Gus arrived and caught the rail of the truck bed and swung himself up lightly, like a much younger man than he was. The host walked away; startled into this new reality by the truck's brief delay, Hamid turned around and looked at Gus sitting there, waiting to go with a placid expression on his face, and an unexplainable hatred turned his insides out.

The emotion drained him. As the truck shuddered along the sandy road and then angled up the pass from the wadi, giving them the first view into Riyadh, Hamid shrank in his seat and knew that the defeat he thought he had banished had won out after all. He had never really fully admitted to it; now he had no choice. His wife kept herself pulled in too but her eyes were keen, her mind registered everything from her place in the back of the truck. On the outskirts of the city were two broad and sumptuous buildings, marbled and shining, with cross-hatched construction roads leading in every direction. After a while the truck bumped up onto a paved avenue, which stretched wide and clean for less than a mile before tilting them out onto roughness again, and now there were more buildings, ramshackle, mixed in with the haphazard beginnings of still more new ones. Chickeny orange and yellow cranes jerked and bobbed across the skyline. The driver turned into the thicket of the city's center and unloaded them next to market stalls where camels stretched themselves down next to trucks and wandered into the street. The bargainers at the stalls were shrill and fast; no one looked up from their business for more than an instant at the three who stood there blinking in the sun, turning their heads back and forth in disorientation. Rafa, her senses growing sharper, knew they would soon be overwhelmed and led them into a smaller street behind a row of sacked wheat. Buildings loomed over them. Gus shouldered their rolled-up rugs and baskets and stayed one step behind Hamid, who was stunned and faltering, opening and closing his hands as if seeking something to grasp. Rafa did not know where she was, or how long they wandered, but soon the glimmer of the newer shops and stalls gave way to more wasted façades. Where light filtered through it was cruel in revelation. She stopped in a narrow alley where the stench of sewage had a muffling effect; the sounds of car horns and shouting were sucked away, and when she listened she heard the voices of women predominating, and those of the grimy children who squatted in the gutter and hung on the broken gates, squalling and shooing at flies.

Yes, she decided.

The next morning, after her first sleep in the flat she would live in for the rest of her life, Rafa checked the air again and this time, the stench carried something else, some kind of promise. She had had nothing to clean with the night before except a withered broom left behind by the previous tenant. She sat up on the rug she'd slept on, vowing to wash the floors. It was still early. She padded softly by Hamid, sleeping on a rug next to her, and he stirred and turned. She roamed through the other two rooms quietly—Gus slept in the front, by the door, looking weightless in repose. The other room was a primitive kitchen, with a metal bin and one tilted shelf nailed crudely to the wall. *So*, she thought. She traced the periphery, marking her spaces. She looked for a long while out the small window above the shelf, where she could see the sun blazing up. It pushed insistently through the pane, which was—wonderfully— quite clean. Rafa waited until the warmth enveloped her face and she had determined everything she must do. When she returned to the room where she'd slept, her husband was dead.

———

August Bartel. Date of birth, 1920. Nationality, American. He knew who he was—he'd never been in doubt since his moment of not dying—but it had taken more time to repair his memories.

There had been the war, of course, though he could not say why he had fought it, but he did remember that fighting was expected of men and that it had taken him away from a home he had never loved. He knew he had not entirely shed his identity as an

American, a Texan—he had used it to intrigue his friend Basim, who had been avoiding his home too. Which of them had convinced the other finally that it was the desert home they should go to was another point on which Gus was unclear. All he could think now was that they had both thought they'd have more room to run.

He knew that Basim had not been his first lover. The war had provided that, in a furtive subterranean way. Gus knew he had been used to the denials; what he had not expected from Basim was his fatalism. When they left Basim's family—Gus recalled his many sisters, his suspicious older brother and especially the proud father, that stately Bedouin chief of the kind Hamid had worked for all his life—he had not at first realized that Basim had every intention of letting the desert swallow them.

He knew also how he had been found. He had not breathed in some time, Hamid told him. There had been a storm. As was often the case, the following day was bright and clear. Hamid and his brother and nephew rode out with the camels to find the desert floor lush with green and flowers. They saw a flash from behind a dune and rode toward it, and over the rise they came to a campsite, which they found flooded through, a jeep tossed on one side by the wind and its cab pushed into the drifts, as if a large hand had held it that way while it filled. A metal pole lay a short distance away where the runoff had formed an alluvial slope. The men surmised that it had been wrenched from a tent, but it was clean of any cloth or ties; it was the sun's glare that had struck it and caught Hamid's notice in the first place. They also detected a mound with more metal jutting through caked sand. They hastened to begin digging, though they expected to find no one any longer living. Hamid pulled a long piece of cloth from the mound. It had not been damaged by anything sharp. The color of the fabric was unfamiliar to him, but, examining the tight weave, he could see that it was sturdy and of some value. Its origin was made clear when the other two, shoveling furiously, exclaimed that they had found someone. Hamid looked; the hair that was revealed on the head of the curled-up figure was light in color. The man was lying on his side and wrapped in a blanket. Another pole—a twin to the one they had found flung away—was wedged over the man's head and had made a small pocket around him. The second body lay next to the first man. Hamid saw one of their own. He had turned to meet his fate, however, and bore the brunt of the drift that had meant to claim them both.

Gus knew that once he and Basim had been freed from the sand, Hamid and his men salvaged what material made itself clear: another tent pole, sharply bent, and a length of rope that did not appear to have been used to tie anything, although it was mud-streaked and wet. A battered drinking flask, a pouch of dates, binoculars, and a metal drinking cup that expanded and collapsed into itself again. The men wrapped these items and tied them onto one of their camel sacks. It was not disrespectful to do this. Much more inexcusable would be to allow these things to remain unused; they would expect nothing less than that others do the same should they themselves succumb in this way. They did not know the man who was of their own kind, but they buried him in a pit and carefully placed rocks over his body until he was secure. The light-haired man was breathing shallowly now that the grains had been wiped from his nose and mouth. Though they did not expect him to live, the men knew that it was their duty to take him with them. God had not finished the work of killing him.

———

Rafa wondered why she had not acknowledged the propulsion toward death—why she had attributed her husband's failures and restless searching to simple male pride. That morning, after finding Hamid lifeless, she reflected that in earlier years, poor and poorer as they became, they had nevertheless been able to rely on the bedu tradition of a host's protection for three days after departing. The belief was that any food ingested took that amount of time to quit the body. *Well*, she thought. Hamid's relation had clearly decided that this tradition was no longer of any importance.

Now Rafa found it easy to eschew some traditions herself. She discovered that here, on this shabby street, she was not the only one. The women's voices she had heard became matched to their faces: the abandoned wives and spinster daughters, the cast-off mistresses and girls who limped or were blind. She made a fast bond with her downstairs neighbor when, pumping water from the rusted spout in the central courtyard, the older woman approached and asked forthrightly who they were. Rafa explained. The woman nodded, as if she'd heard a story like this one before, and then efficiently arranged for Hamid's body to be removed by two young men who shuffled from the dim recesses of the yard when she called to them. They were her grandsons—"Twins, both idiots," she said to Rafa, and shrugged. Their identical faces were sullen and slack. Rafa watched them climb up the metal rungs to the second floor. When Gus emerged into the courtyard, assisting the boys in getting Hamid's swaddled form into the back of a wagon, the woman said, in her matter-of-fact voice, "At least you have only one on your hands now."

The street pulsed with this life. Rafa's immediate concern was money: something that she had never handled before, and that Hamid had had little of even after working harvests or living off his host's largesse. She sorted through the collection of clothing and utensils she'd salvaged from Al-Kharj and turned her bitterness toward that indolent wife into industry. There was washing work—she found the street where the maids of the rich doled out the clothing of their employers, Saudis of the new kind who would soon live in walled-off villas but were in hotels, for now, where there was not enough help to go around. It was laughable, Rafa thought: the city was exploding too fast. Oil—this new term she learned—did indeed trickle its way down, and while the rich waited for their indoor plumbing to be installed she and the other women carried basket after basket of fine fabrics on their heads, back to their forgotten little street where the washed garments hung to dry, and then, folded and stacked, were returned each evening to the Filipino and

Thai girls who would not look them in the face when they paid. These foreign servants left their heads bare, but Rafa and the other washers did not—until they had turned the last corner into their street again, a crumbled entry behind rows of construction bins that was unnoticeable to most passersby. Once there, propriety did not concern them.

The neighbor woman was Rafa's inspiration, and she eyed Gus now with disdain, and spoke to him little except to adopt a tone of command. She sent him on errands and directed him very precisely—she seemed to have imprinted a map of the rapidly changing city in her head—to sites where buildings were being razed or built, and counted the riyals he brought back. Like the other men of the street, Gus was superfluous. "Not worth what they bring in," Rafa soon learned to agree, when she cooked with the other women in the evenings at the brick-ringed fire in the courtyard. The men sidled in from a day's work like unhappy shadows. They took what the women gave them to eat, and sat against the peeling paint of the far wall while Rafa and the others plotted out chores and traded stories.

And Gus was paid less than other men. Sometimes—he could not bear to tell Rafa—he was not hired at all; he would arrive early with the other laborers, just as the sun was glowing on the horizon, and the foremen looked at the strange figure he presented with skepticism. He wore a thobe, and wrapped his head like the others; his skin was colored deep from his years out of doors, but his light eyes and wispy, golded beard stubble made him look like a man lost. Occasionally they approached him and spoke to him in English, which was worse, as he could not reply. He might be given a broom and told to sweep, or jerry cans of water to refill and carry to the other workers. But more often, when he answered their inquiries in the bedu tongue, he was simply sent away. He could not tell Rafa this. When he was let go he began his own wanderings, imprinting his own map of what he saw. The city was omnivorous. The construction was eating into the desert, new streets and buildings digesting another spread of it week by week. Gus walked to where the market stalls had been; they were never the same, undulating in different patterns each day and spreading out from the mosque and clock tower and gradually, into covered-over lanes with glass fronts and tiles. The cars were greedy, driving over construction blockades and onto sidewalks, their drivers impatient for access and speed. There were office buildings, ministries, sprawling villas. The noise from all of this was astounding to Gus. It dredged up recollections of other places he might have been. Here too he began to see people who were not of this place, but they were also not of his time. One day, after piling scrap metal into a truck for six hours (the money would perhaps please Rafa, he thought, or at least he hoped), he turned into the corridors behind the Friday mosque where sleek young Saudi men stood behind counters selling gold. The chains and ingots hung in thick coils from hooks on the walls, and the counter cases held a bounty of glowing pendants, breastplates, and rings. At one stall two ruddy men wearing checked shirts and denims pushed ring after ring onto their sunburned fingers. One of them found what he wanted—it was a heavy whorl of gold in tones of umber, rose, and white—and reached into the back pocket of his jeans to retrieve a wallet so stuffed with riyal bills that they spilled out onto the floor behind him.

"Aw, shit," the man said. When he turned more bills fluttered to the ground. This made his companion laugh. "There goes your Monopoly money," he said, and his friend laughed too.

Gus had been standing off to the side, watching the transaction; the men had paid him no attention. Now he reached down and gathered the scattered bills. He handed them to the man and nodded once, starting to move off as if he had just been passing by on his way to somewhere else.

The man looked him over, then laughed again with his friend. "Thanks, Cap'n!" he said to Gus. Then, "Hell of an outfit you've got there—sorry I missed the party."

"Yeah," Gus found himself saying. It came out in the drawl of his childhood. "Sure was," he said. "Yeah." He smiled, out of words to offer up.

It was enough for the men—they laughed again, and one of them slapped him on the back and said "Woo-ee!" while the other made a tippling motion with his hand and winked. "Well, you don't smell like it," he said.

That was the beginning. There had been no more to the conversation—Gus had walked away, the men had seemed to think nothing amiss—and in the women's street that night he reported nothing of the encounter to Rafa. At the cooking fire she was animatedly talking with her neighbor and did not look up when Gus handed her his money, and so she missed the new spark behind his eyes. In the days and weeks that followed Gus found more opportunities to exchange speech with the foreigners he saw in the souks. Small words sufficed—"hey" and "howdy there" (there were a number of these expatriates from the western and southern states, Gus discovered). Now and then, something about how hot it was. Or the price of gold. When Gus had these exchanges no one seemed overly curious about his clothing; in fact there were others of his kind dressed this way too, the ones eager to appear like experts. It was 1974. Gus reacquainted himself with the Western calendar by saving a riyal here and there from what he earned, until he had enough to buy a small datebook that he kept in the pocket of his thobe along with his long-expired passport. *August Bartel. Date of birth, 1920.*

When he'd been rescued he had said nothing at all for weeks, longer perhaps—that was when time had changed for him. His body made its own decision, and his tongue was simply part of it. The language he began to speak, when he did speak, was one he knew not to be his own, but he understood it. He'd been dimly aware, too, of some idea that this predicament of learning to talk and to understand was something that had been experienced by others, and that he had heard this somehow, when he was young. Later, he would remember books; there his mind played tricks with him too, for when he remembered these adventures of others it seemed as if he knew so many of them, when in fact he had not been much of a reader at all. Now, at the building sites, he could initiate as well as respond. He trusted that a new word would come from his lips when it was ready to; he didn't force them to come out if they were not. He was hired more often. Bringing home this money won him at least a semblance of appreciation from Rafa. Once, when he arrived home later than the other men and presented his earnings in a roll of colorful riyal bills (the bank, too, was a place he had found to converse), she gave out a tiny smile, a flicker of a smile, a tired look that traveled in that brief moment across the years in the desert and Al-Kharj to where they were now. The old neighbor woman was sitting in her usual place next to Rafa. Seeing the bills, she shook a gnarled finger and scolded, "If he's stealing, it's his hand, you know." Gus said, "*La!*"—so forcefully that the word seemed to sear itself into the air. His own word—*No*—simmered and died in his mouth. Now Rafa's look was wary, and for the first time since their arrival in the city, Gus knew, she was assessing where her loyalties should lie. But the moment passed, and that night Rafa gave him one more tight smile, out of sight of the other woman, but nothing more was insinuated and Gus continued to be paid well—for a laborer—and day after day he gave his money to Rafa and their time in the street of women went on. Rafa's suspicion was not the problem between them. *We could continue like this,* Gus thought, *forever.* The problem was that Gus could not get his fill of words from the building sites in the city, or from speaking with other Westerners in the streets. In the courtyard at night he was stifled. He continued to tell Rafa nothing. He was terrified that he would one day become uncontrollably garrulous, and that it would happen in the wrong place, in the wrong tongue. And twinned with his new lust for language came the resurgence of physical desire—it was the thing that had been buried the longest, and it was tumultuous, enveloping him sometimes so suddenly and violently on a street corner in the souks that he would have to wrap his arms around his body in restraint, and he could not tell which would betray him first: his words or his hands.

When Rafa ignored him in the courtyard at night he found himself flushed, watching her, as he had never felt with any woman, and he saw the way Rafa's hips moved underneath her abayah when she turned to poke down the fire, or in the flat, when she bent to shake out a rug. There seemed to be still a rounded shape to her, something alive and sinuous. He tried to recall her younger form but of course he had never seen it; he did now remember, though, how Hamid would call to her on some nights in the desert, and when he did how Rafa would retreat behind the dividing curtain in the tent. A full moon or dying embers from the fire might illuminate the curtain and trace the edge of her reclining shape. Hamid would lay a hand on the rise of it and she would turn to her stomach, her face pressed into the rug. The recollection of Rafa's shape and Hamid's guiding hand was sharp with meaning for Gus. What was he doing? he asked himself. He had never desired her. She was the same as she had ever been, but now her flank seemed to throw off a scent for him—it clawed into his nostrils and upset his balance.

He saw men in the street—young Saudis in blinding white thobes, holding hands—and his desire experienced another seismic shift. This time the wrench in his gut bent him over. An American boy in a baseball cap walked by with a man who looked to be his father, dressed in a military uniform of the kind Gus had seen more and more of. A thread of nausea looped through him. He bought a bottle of water from a tall Somali woman who sold them from a tub (*Don't look at her, don't look*, he cautioned himself), and retreated to a shaded step behind the market stalls to sit down. He was clammy. Were either speech or desire refound, he wondered, if he could do nothing with them?

He would always know that he never laid a hand on her. He knew he should not try, and he knew his desire was misdirected— that afternoon as he sat there, sickened with himself, he was able to admit the direction his body would lead him again, and it would be into different streets, another place, a myriad of faceless men. That night when he returned to the courtyard he took his meal as he had other nights, sitting back and saying nothing. Later in the flat he told Rafa, *I cannot go through this again*, and other things Basim had said to him on their last night in the desert together. *I am guilty*, Basim had said. *When I think about it I feel guilty and scared and ashamed.*

Telling Rafa, his words tumbled out in English and Gus knew she could not understand them—but she might have discerned what he meant.

———

He had never touched her, though he had wanted to simply lay a hand on her shoulder—*Thank you,* he might have said, in her language. Despite the heat of that night when he left the flat for good, he wished that he had. But that was not the way it had gone. When Rafa responded to his long speech she had been in a fury— what else had he kept hidden from her? It was no use to try and explain, as he did not understand it himself. He hadn't known which words to use. He had even wept, he remembered: they both had, a thing between them that seemed as impossible an occurrence then as it did now. He would learn to touch intimately again, in the years that followed, but it would never be a comfort in the way that the imagined touch with Rafa would have been.

There were things he learned to avoid as time went on. *August Bartel*—no, he would never leave. He could not. Detection grew less and less of a threat, and he moved more easily as the city melted down its boundaries. There were other forgotten streets to sleep in where the police never went. The Westerners drifted through Riyadh and left again, after making their money; Gus slid from one job to another without the required papers and added more to the vocabulary of his once-lost language, terms such as "independent contractor" that seemed to answer all questions and leave no trace.

One more jolt occurred, though this time it did not shake him as the others had. He'd retained songs in his head, all along— those odd melodies, the ones from dances Hamid had tried to describe to his friend in Al-Kharj. Gus accepted easily this last old part of himself when it welled up, just as he needed a bit more money to get by: the role of a Texan. The expatriates of the city were restless, and drank too much. They did things for entertainment that they might never have done back home. And so Gus, presuming on an acquaintance from a building site at the Army Corps of Engineers, was hired as a caller for the square dances that these people got up as one more way to stave off boredom and sleep with other people's wives. *Shoot that star, left allemande, gonna pass your partner by*—it all came back. He'd been raised on a farm and these were the country dances of his youth, the time before he knew why he was nervous and jittery with his partners, before he'd run away to fly planes in the war and never returned. *Hey corner box the gnat then you do-si-do.* Everyone could get the do-si-do or the daisy chain; there would be a lot of laughing and missed steps for the rest of the night, but no one seemed to mind. In the thobe and ghotra, standing there with his eyes half-closed as he called out the steps, the dancers wondered who this man was but they accepted him as just one more character who would pass through and leave again. He led them into a cloverleaf, through the Grand Q, the wagon wheel and dip and dive. The grand tour was last—*now ladies face to back up four*—and for thirty-two beats they went on, Gus knowing that his commands were perfect, that every couple he'd split at the beginning of the sequence would end up together again.

Your body makes the decisions for you, he told himself. In a dance you simply followed; all it took was the caller's surety, and everyone would fall into line without thinking. The desert made the body want nothing more than water. You could go on for a long time without food—sometimes, when a harvest had been especially bad or when livestock died, he and Rafa and Hamid had existed for weeks by sucking grease from preserved dates or dissolving shards of dried camel's milk on their tongues. You simply told yourself that you would survive on it, and you did. In the desert his body had made the decision to expel sand from his throat and let him breathe again; instead of relinquishing life, he had given up feeling instead. Breath, or a full heart. He hadn't even made the choice.

———

By the late 1980s the city's mood had shifted again. Glass and steel towers brushed the sky, and roads spun around themselves and dove into tunnels. Neon light pulsed from glossy shopping malls and even the vendors selling schwarmas had been forced into spruced-up shacks, where the lights made the meat rotisseries gleam as they turned slowly, as if resisting. Anyone catching sight of a camel these days would imagine that a circus had come to town. It had been over three years since Riyadh had been startled by bombs —at a pizza shop and a Kentucky Fried Chicken, both protests against Westernization in which no one had been hurt—but after that the tightening began.

Gus was questioned once, by a prowling muttawein—his age (respect of elders was a tradition still) got him off without incident. The redbeard had been rude at first—he'd caught Gus eating when the shops were closed for prayers—but then deferential when he answered his questions smoothly in Arabic. No, he was not drunk. Yes, he was employed by Prince Mohammed.

That had been a risk—he was not employed by anyone, not legally. He still picked up work but his age wasn't helping him. Outside of the expatriates' villas and compounds, where he could still sweep or water gardens or answer telephones, he could not compete with the lithe young men from India or Malaysia who would work faster and for less, and who had the official documents.

He still called dances. The night after the questioning he arrived at a new company compound where the swimming pool was rigged with spiraling waterslides and the wives had their own gymnasium, where they were forced to keep the curtains pulled over the floor-to-ceiling windows so that they could not be seen when they exercised. These same women wore long cotton dresses when Gus saw them in the shopping malls or the souks, abayahs trailing them like an afterthought. Behind the walls of the compound they donned trousers so snug they revealed every bump and line, bared their shoulders in shirts with strips of fabric criss-crossing their exposed, suntanned backs, and tugged shiny material across their limbs that pulled up in the crotch when they went to the gym. Sometimes these sartorial changes that had occurred over the years confounded Gus—women had outfitted themselves much more demurely even outside of these walls, outside of this world, when he had been young, and he had missed some evolutionary link from then to now that would explain the get-ups he saw. At the compound the dancing was delayed that night—there was a party first, a birthday. "Ah hell," he was told by one of the regular dancers, a man he'd seen around for the past year or so. "I didn't know. It's our V.P., though—the guy's turning seventy, for Chrissakes, so there's nothing we can do." Gus sat in a folding chair in the back of the recreation hall where the compound residents gathered. The men were freshly combed, the women loud and sassy. Here and there a few children—the older teenagers who had been dragged to this country with their families and existed on deep sufferance—skulked around a table in the back, pilfering wine when the Egyptian barman wasn't looking.

Suddenly the lights in the room dimmed, and from somewhere a spotlight was directed at the curtained stage up in front—there were movies shown here too, Gus remembered, once having arrived on the wrong night and stumbled into a viewing of a picture involving men with guns and a good deal of facial hair. Now the curtain parted to reveal two men dressed in clown suits. They placed a tape recorder on the stage in front of them and waved. They audience hooted and cheered. The spotlight jerked into the front row—the honoree smiled gamely, a still vigorous-looking man with deeply tanned skin—and as the lighting technician tried to find the stage again, the spotlight careening from one side to the other, Gus saw one of the clowns—he was losing his pants and laughing at something—push a button on the tape recorder. Music blared out across the stage. *Our Father, Who art in heaven, Hallowed be Thy name, Thy kingdom come, Thy will be done, On earth as it is in heaven.* It was a woman's voice. The chorus repeated over and over and it had an electric sound, guitars and drums and a steady beat. *On earth as it is in he-eh-ah-ehven*—everyone in the hall clapped and sang along. The clowns jumped off the stage and began passing out balloons, silver and pink and blue and red, and they jiggled from people's hands and bounced out of time with the song and floated up to the ceiling, where the strings and ribbons made their own rhythm

—meandering and sad, unconnected to the clapping and stomping below.

As Gus left the song was still going on—or being replayed—and only the occasional word reverberated into the night. *Will. Done. EARTH as it is in HE-eh-ah-ehVEN.* The compound was otherwise still; he left through the gate and the young guard, a Saudi boy, shot his eyes over to him and then quickly back, as if he'd seen an apparition. It was a mild night and the air was balmy. Gus walked for some time through the maze of quiet side streets, forcing himself not to rush. He would not anticipate, he thought. When he found the entryway to the old street he felt uneasy at how exactly the same it appeared: the chink in the plaster at the arch, the bins with scrap metal and insulation still shoved in front of it like retired sentries. He had not been back to the flat, or seen Rafa again, since that night when he had not touched her, when he had said the wrong things and too much. He had expected, perhaps, to find the street gone—consumed by the city. It was not. The sky was dark now, and the city's glow obscured any stars, and on the street yellowish pools of light from recently installed street lamps—already fitzing and neglected—led him to Rafa's building. It had been given a fresh coat of paint, but it still leaned into the house next to it, as if to prop it up. The courtyard was there, and the fire, and so was she.

She was older, of course. Looking at the cluster of women seated around the fire—the bricks had stayed the same, too—Gus saw that Rafa was the oldest one among them, her hair threaded with gray and uncovered, pulled back in a long braid that trailed down the back of her abayah. The old neighbor woman was not there (she had died, Gus supposed, correctly). In her place was a man who looked to be nearing middle age; it was difficult to tell, as his body was filled out but unmatched to the expression on his face, which was soft and trusting but grew tense as Gus approached.

Rafa said to the man, who was visibly agitated now, that it was all right, he did not have to worry. This simple reassurance calmed him immediately. Turning to Gus, Rafa explained that the other twin had died—so this was one of the boys who had taken Hamid away, Gus realized, carted him out to the edge of the city where the poor were covered over with rocks until their resting place was covered over by something else. If the twin understood he was being talked about he gave no sign; he seemed content again with the state of things, humming as he picked bits of food from his bowl.

"He's clung to me ever since," Rafa said sadly. "It's been a long time."

It was not easy. Trading stories would be difficult, and they would need to find a way to begin. Gus sat on the ground so that Rafa could see his face if she wanted to, read his eyes as best she could in the flameglow. He offered first only a description of that very night—the clowns and the balloons, the clapping hands and strange, inappropriate clothing—and Rafa listened, murmuring only the occasional "yes" or "I see" in reply. This beginning would have to do. The rest would come in fits and starts. Gus let the bedu words come out smoothly, continuously, but his voice was soft and measured and he paused now and then to let her nod or say "yes" again. The other women gathered up the dishes and moved away. Gus kept talking. Rafa said little, but she did not tell him to leave. They found it difficult to look at one another for very long, but when this was the case they watched the lone twin, who refused to leave Rafa's side, and continued his private humming as sparks from the fire cracked and ashed into the night. He would outlive them both.

HAYLOADER

Three weeks into June, and the Sri Lankans all want to know when they're getting their vacations. I drive out to the canteen a little late, at a quarter past six. Usually we're going by five or so, to get a half-day in before the heat comes up on us. Today when I walk in they all look up from their breakfasts and stop talking. The pure shit-dinginess of this place is a thousand times worse when it's quiet: the fake wood paneling on the walls seems to stare right back at you, the plastic chairs and card tables shift and the linoleum tiles creak, and the one window, with its view straight out into sand-locked nowhere, wheezes in its frame. Back in the kitchen, the stove coughs and there's the thud of the freezer case that Bo has to weigh down with supply boxes so it will stay shut. He's working on lunch now, trying to make time in case the generator goes out again.

I go over to the tray of eggs and potatoes, shovel what's left of the mess onto a plate and sit at the small table in the corner. When we started up three years back it was just Robbie and me, sitting in here—Sheikh Halim gave orders that the workers should pick their food up from the window. They didn't seem to mind.

"Mister Todd," one of them says now. I can tell they've been waiting. The way they wait is almost regal—like I'm here to do something for them. I wish I could tell him what I know he wants to hear, but I can't. "Mister Todd," he says again. "We wonder—"

"I haven't heard from the sheikh, P.J.," I say quickly. I don't say that I don't know if the sheikh's in Riyadh, or even in the country. It's all I can do to meet the eyes of the expectant group of men sitting there. *Mister.* Like I've done anything to earn it, aside from being the white guy who's running things, although the Sri Lankans know better than that.

P.J. nods, and looks like he's about to say something else but doesn't. He wipes his fingers on the end of the turban that trails from his head. The rest of the men go back to their plates, spooning up the greasy bits around the rims as if that's just what they'd been waiting to do.

P.J. isn't P.J., and by now he probably knows that he's the third guy to come through in as many years of crews who's been bestowed with that moniker. For that matter, Bo isn't Bo—although he picked the name, when he saw that we weren't ever going to be able to get our brains around his. He figured us out quick. Maybe because he's been here the longest—since we got the farm started up in '83— he feels comfortable coming out and clapping twice, politely, to let the crew know that it's time to move along. They file out to the fields, where I know they'll be cursing the sheikh, and me.

While Bo moves around collecting the plates in a trash bag, I wonder whether Cal's been able to raise Halim from the land line in Al-Kharj and when the hell anyone's going to give me a hint as to what's going on. Last month when harvest was about to start the sheikh trotted out a whole merry entourage of his friends to bear witness to the glory of fertilization we'd made happen in the middle of the desert. All credit to him, of course. Although it was a bit ridiculous—we'd had a rare rain, and the rich city Saudis were splashing through the mud puddles like kids, thobes hiked up around their knees—I had to admit to myself that it looked pretty grand. Amber waves of grain, and all that, making the view from the red-rock escarpments look like golden silk on the desert floor for as far as you could see. I remember thinking that it was too bad Dee Dee never got to see it like that.

"There's this today too, Mister Todd," Bo's saying. I look up and he's standing by the table with a plate of bacon.

"Hey, well that's great," I say.

"Water buffalo," he says, shrugging casually. "You know."

"Thanks," I say. The stuff's actually all right: if you can't get pork, for some reason the canned water buffalo from India—labeled simply "beef," which gave Dee Dee a shock when she read the fine print—ends up tasting like the closest thing to it. Bo does something with the spices before he fries it.

He says he has to talk to me too, and joins me at the table where I'm sitting. Here's where I should say that Bo is probably the best-looking member of the human species that I have ever seen. Don't get me wrong. Even out here, without decent female company, it's not like I'm about to make the switch to the other team. It really just doesn't happen here like you might think it would. But Bo's beauty is ridiculous: the finest bones, lips like a high-school sweetheart-cum-porn star, skin that looks like it's dusted with gold powder even when the rest of us are sweating like hogs.

I chew on the bacon and he tells me pretty much what I'm expecting. Of course I know that he is very happy here. He has been happy to be here since the beginning, when it was nothing and now it's something. It is not a problem that so many different crews come through here, from all over the world, wanting food he has to improvise from a limited supply. No. And it is not the money, not really. But he thinks that maybe it is the right time to take another job, what with things feeling uncertain. "My wife can come," he says. "It is not so much more money, but if it is guaranteed then I will be able to bring her."

I try to imagine what the wife looks like: probably just as beautiful. More. They'll have the most ethereal, gorgeous children on the planet.

"Where?" I ask him.

He waits a beat at this, looking down a bit uncomfortably. "Well," he says. With his impeccable manners, this might take him awhile. He shifts in the chair and the early sunray coming in through the smudged window falls across his face, and now he can't lie. "Over at Mister Cal's," he says. "It's—very much larger place."

"Yeah. That it is." Bo gives me a wan smile. What a bastard Cal is, I'm thinking. Now I know for sure I'm on a sinking ship.

Bo gets up. "Sheikh Halim will call you soon?" he asks. I say I'm sure he will and Bo nods and backs away deferentially, as if any of this is going to make a difference.

I grab the rest of the bacon in my hand and go outside. Standing on the steps of the trailer is like being a very primitive king surveying his fiefdom: the way the desert slopes and pitches, you don't need a rise any higher than the one we're staked up on to get a good feel for the land. At seven in the morning in June there's still that last bit of cool wearing off in the air. Since it's technically still spring the brutal haze won't come until a bit later; for now I can see acres of field stretching away, the mist from the watering pivots giving the unharvested plots a last drizzle, and the reaped parts—that's most of it by now—looking rich and brown and ready to turn under again. The fields are ringed by escarpments, and we haven't needed the fences since Sheikh Halim paid the Bedouin off to move farther out into the desert. They no longer graze their sheep and camels on the seed sprout. I can see a group of nomad women, though, squatting at the base of the rocks a quarter-mile off. They're scanning the scene like I am, deciding when they can gather what's left over from the piles of wheat we've moved. We leave them alone; it's a truce of sorts.

I can still look at all this, sometimes, and think how we made it from nothing.

———

One more time with the combine. There's just the far north fields left to clear, and we've only been delaying for the sake of giving the men some more work to do while we wait: Sheikh Halim still refuses to pay them on salary, and compensates each man by the hour. "Never the fuck mind," Robbie said before he left last year, "that we'd all have shorter goddamn days if they knew they could knock off after getting it done." I haven't had the chance to revisit the issue since I've been on my own again.

Efram still hasn't gotten used to the machine. If you do it right you can clear a field in four hours, but he'll spend half that just maneuvering back and forth, back and forth, and getting it stuck in good between the muddy pivot tracks. The other guys are there to help out: Manuel shouting directions, Jimmy and Rico moving the pivots out of the way and getting doused with water when one of them unexpectedly spurts. Rico's quick to address anything mechanical that can go wrong and will—just this one field will take them all day.

The Sri Lankans, meanwhile, are piling up the harvested grain from the other fields, stacking it high on tarps. We're going to have to pray there isn't a freak spring storm to soak through the top layers while it sits there. Bo has taken a break from the canteen and stands between the fields, watching the scene with a grin. He thinks the Mexicans are hilarious: "No can fucking drive, eh?" he'll say to me sometimes. "How many for screw in light bulb?" He tries to talk to them though, evenings, to find out what he can do to the food to make them like it. Maybe they don't know how to farm in sand, but it's not like Bo came out here knowing he'd have to cook the way he does, either.

A dirt plume barreling down the road in the distance has got to be Cal. When he pulls up he swerves the truck to a stop like he's skiing it, one hand on the wheel. He's scratching the back of his neck with the other.

"There you are," he says. As if I might be anywhere else. He steps out of the truck. It's an oversized Ford, one of those models that looks like it belongs in a dust bowl film. Cal's six-feet-six and managed to convince Sheikh Halim that no way was he going to be able to fold himself into a white Toyota pickup like everyone else.

"You heard from Halim?" I ask him. When he sighs and walks over, he takes his hand away from his neck and wipes blood on his jeans.

"What the hell did you do now," I say.

"Fucking sand fly." He ducks his head around to show me the sore, red and angry and oozing pus.

"Jesus, Cal, that's looking rude."

He shrugs: he'll probably just let it fester for awhile, until it gets so bad he has to lance it or it just dries up. Cal thinks there's a certain level of disgusting shit you should just be able to deal with out here. He prides himself on it. Back when Robbie and I first got here, when we found out Halim hadn't even bothered to have anyone assemble our trailers, we slept in a tent for a month. When we complained about the scorpions and tarantulas we had to beat back all night, Cal told us that we were bigger pussies than any Bedouin girl he'd seen.

His words did have an effect, but who knew how far we'd go to prove it?

I know from the way Cal's staring off at the workers that there's stuff he's not telling me. Why, for example, Sheikh Halim hasn't sent out the appraiser to calculate the worth of the harvest, and why I've been summoned twice, late at night, to drive the sixty miles to Al-Kharj to await a phone call from Halim that hasn't come. The crop's piling up and there's no money coming in—not for any of us. No wonder Bo wants to bail out.

"Looking good," Cal says. "Real good, Todd. This place is finally getting up to speed, producing something."

I say, "You want to cut the shit here, Cal? That's sounding like a golden handshake, if you know what I mean."

"That isn't it," he says.

"Then you want to tell me what?"

"I'm going to." He's cool about it: meaning, whatever it is, it's a done deal, something he's worked out with Halim that he now has to pass on to me.

"All right," he says, "it's like this. You don't have the silos up out here—"

"No shit," I say. "And whose fault is that? Halim told those guys from Texas to fuck off after one month. No way was it going to get done."

"I know it, I know it," he says, keeping his voice level. "But since all that happened"—and here he looks at me carefully—"Halim's decided to put it up in the silos at my place. There's room and we'll be able to wait out the glut until the goddamned Agricultural Ministry figures their shit out."

I wonder how the Sri Lankans are going to feel, having to load up everything they've just stacked and then unload it again into the silos. Looking out at the dull gold piles, taking on a reddish hue as we get on toward the higher noon sun, I calculate: three days.

"They need to get paid," I say. "They want their leave."

"It'll happen. Halim's releasing the funds and everyone's passports just as soon as it's stored and he knows what he'll get for it."

"And I need to get paid, Cal. It's not like Halim doesn't have the money. You know this is bullshit. I spec'd out the yield last fall the way he wanted it—screw the surplus problem."

"Halim's in the same position as everyone else," Cal says. "Ain't like he's gonna get a special audience with the king about it." I'm supposed to laugh at this, but I don't so Cal says, "Fahad, His Royal Highness, that fat fuck," and laughs himself.

He walks back to over to the truck and takes a paper bag out from under the front seat. "Here," he says, tossing it to me. "Christmas in June. Robbie's coming down for the weekend, and I'm bringing my crew, and we'll let them blast through the work and pay them overtime and make one last big party of it." I look in the bag: no surprise, it's a brick of hash the size of an Ivory soap bar.

"What else," I say.

Cal pats the back of his neck again, coming away this time with a smear of yellow in the blood. "Shit. I guess it's infected," he says, laughing. "Got your jackknife on you?"

I take it off my belt and whip the blade open. "Just a sec, here," Cal says. He reaches under the seat again and pulls out a bottle, takes a big gulp and splashes some of the liquid on the sore. He hands over the bottle and I start to shake my head.

"Come on, Todd—code of the desert," he says. "Gentlemen's honor."

"Fuck you."

I take it and the pure one-hundred-eighty-proof's like a spear in my throat. But I'm glad I've swallowed it when I cut into the bite on his neck: the blade slices distended purpling flesh, and a mess of infection gushes out all over my hand and down the back of Cal's checkered shirt. "*That's* it," he shouts. "Goddamn!" He takes another swig and wipes his neck with the stuff again, making a big show of hollering and pounding the sand with his boot.

I wipe the blade off on the seat of his truck. "What else," I say. "There's something. You'd best just tell me."

He climbs back into the driver's seat, holding a dirty torn ghotra rag to the draining wound. "Consolidation," he says. "Halim wants one farm—diversification, he wants grass, he wants alfalfa— this one'll be under mine, all the crew based there." He starts the engine. "Look—I'm working it out so there's still a place for you. You know that."

All this, all this. Cal's squinting in that wise-man pose he likes to take, though I guess he's earned it after all these years out here, making his way. He looks like an old cowboy who's genuinely sorry that I'm the punk who has to get screwed.

"Get my money," I yell as he rolls up the window and guns the motor. He nods and goes from zero to sixty in record time as he heads back to the main road.

—

I toss the hash brick into my bottom dresser drawer with the wool sweaters I'm not wearing this time of year. I'll know it's there, but I won't have to look at it tonight. Not that Cal would mind if I chipped a piece off and smoked myself into oblivion: better than getting amped up on my own, which I've done too many times before on coke. He came back once after he'd been gone a week and took one look at me, then said, "Jesus fucking Christ, Todd—that was supposed to be for the next *month,* you know?" There had been a sandstorm that lasted for days, and I'd been stuck out here with no truck while Robbie hunkered down in Riyadh. By the time Cal got out to me it wasn't clear who was the bigger banshee, the storm or me: while it sailed ice and rain down furiously, making the trailer groan and shake, I'd gone half-mad tearing up the carpet to have something to do. The windows were blasted over with red sand and I couldn't see out. I'd scratched marks into the living room paneling to track the time.

Sometimes I just refuse to keep the stuff, and I let Cal think it's because I need to come down from the jag and sober up but it's a different kind of clearing I'm after. I'll spend the whole weekend on the rim of the escarpment by day, looking for signs of some other life. Nights I'll confront the cracked walls inside the trailer and think aloud. Out here you always think that it just might come to you. You just might sit and try to find things to listen to and let the silence do its work, let it tell you something about where you are. Maybe, even, if you sit out here long enough, some higher voice will come out of nowhere, and tell you what the hell you should do.

——

Robbie is the Man with the Plan. Turns out, he lied his ass off to get here, not that he felt one second's shame over it. He's from Virginia, like me; we both showed up the same day at some hotel out by Dulles Airport for the interview with Sheikh Halim's missive, and Robbie's so smooth he has us both convinced he's seen and done it all, farm-wise. Halim's guy was skinny and bald. He wore a suit in shiny tan wool and a huge diamond ring, no joke. His head, minus the customary ghotra, was pale pink. You could tell he couldn't wait to get out of that room and out on the town: he took at least four calls while we sat there, all to arrange where "the nice young ladies" would be for the evening. He couldn't have known less about who to hire for a farm. So Robbie filled him in. Only later—months later, actually—did I realize that everything Robbie told him was a souped-up version of the scant details I'd provided to *him* while we waited for the interview.

But Rob was cool: he did the work. He had to be told what to do—sure, maybe he'd done a little bush-hogging one summer, that was it—but he managed it. I couldn't say that I faulted him too much for stretching the truth about his qualifications. It's not like I didn't do a little stretching myself: *sure thing—sand, clay, whatever. It'll work.* Robbie and I both convinced Halim's guy. The Man with the Plan—Rob said it a lot. It might sound stupid, but sometimes in a place like this hearing something familiar over and over sounds good; it makes you think you know someone. Robbie had plans. And talking about them sure didn't hurt his chances of getting laid, when he had the opportunity.

Me, I'm just the foil. My plans were a little money, Dee Dee, a few years out here and then we'd go back home. You've heard this one before, right?

Here's Robbie, hauling seed off the back of a truck, joking around with the first crew we had, Sri Lankans all, in pidgin Arabic and English and whatever else made them laugh. At that point we were both a little giddy with our good luck, which seemed to come in spades after that first awful month of not knowing how we'd ever make it. Halim was practically throwing money at us at that point. Here's Robbie picking up the sandy dirt in his hands: he smells it, declares it'll bring a bounty. Everyone laughs and agrees. A month later, when one of the crew—our first P.J.—wants to quit, Robbie tries sweet-talking him and when that doesn't work, says he's sorry, but he can't find the guy's passport.

And here's Robbie pulling the lid off the septic tank; it's always backing up, and there's no one else to deal with it. There's a tool to pry the lid off but Robbie heaves and tries to yank it. The muscles on his back are huge by now. When he gets it halfway open he lets out a bull-like yell and it slides into the sand. "Dumb as a box of rocks," Cal mutters, watching. "But he works hard." He's shaking his head when he says this, but he can't hide his admiration.

Robbie says, "Down the shithole!" He's gone.

He starts taking off for a day or two, here and there, and we're understanding. Cal's around a lot these early days, supervising —it's his head on the line, with Halim—and anyway Cal's married and my wife's on the way just as soon as we get things really going strong. Every time Rob comes back he makes a big production out of working round the clock, fueled with coke and amphetamines. The day I pick Dee Dee up from the airport we get to the farm at six in the morning—the flights in arrive at all ass-end hours—and here's Robbie, out in the fields, screwing a sprinkler back on to the pivot. "Camel knocked it off," he says when we walk over. He gives Dee Dee a bashful smile while he looks her freely up and down. She fingers the little gold cross hanging around her neck, like she's just remembered it.

And Robbie, later, with the parties he'd get up for us, the women he'd drive hours away to get and then leave stranded out here until he drove them back home. He's good-looking; maybe that's it. Or it's the taste for adventure those girls have, any adventure, when you realize that the exotic they promised you doesn't provide enough adventure on its own. Here's Robbie in his trailer, where he's built a rendition of a tiki bar in the front room and thrown pillows around the floor by the television. We're watching a video he's rented, which sucks power we need out of the generator, but with the booze and the lines Robbie's supplied we hardly care. The movie is awful —some cheap sci-fi thing starring grown-up Erin Moran from *Happy Days*, only here she's unhappy because her space crew is getting picked off one by one, and when a crew member with an ugly face but a hot body is raped by a giant space slug, it's funny. I look over at Rob, laughing his ass off; he's lying on the floor next to a girl with big teased bangs and fuchsia lipstick. There's an afghan over her legs and Rob's hand is under it, right in the vee of her crotch, and the girl is squirming while she concentrates on the screen where the space crew girl is now completely naked, covered with the giant slug's semen while it fucks her to death.

And here is Robbie in the kitchen of my trailer at four in the afternoon on a workday, talking to Dee Dee. By now, six months in, she knows the ropes out here: she's given up jeans on hot days and keeps those long cotton Indian-print dresses to throw on over her shorts or miniskirts. She sunbathes sometimes, in a lawn chair out in front of the door, when it's late morning and she knows that none of the men will be around. She's brown as a nut. Afternoons she's got her Jane Fonda tapes, and even if she looks a bit silly with leg warmers around her ankles the workouts really do something for her thighs. The leg warmers match her shiny pink leotard, cut high, a uniform she refuses to give up half a world away. She's been out in the sun again—the strap marks are redder around the edges —and when I come in she's stretching one leg behind her, hands on her hips. I smell something she's baked: another activity she's latched onto.

"Looking for you," Robbie says right away, when I walk in.

Dee Dee takes her time glancing around to me, her face set in an expression of boredom.

So I think nothing of it, not really. Even if there might be other little signs that Dee Dee isn't quite as happy as she says. There's a party that night, people in from the city: our bona fide cure for all the boredom we pretend we're not facing. We all get fucked up once again and Robbie's experiencing a personal record, taking one girl into the bedroom for awhile and after she passes out, pulling another onto his lap back in the living room, daring her to say anything about his messed-up hair and untucked shirt. This girl doesn't say anything to him but she starts leaning over to whisper in my ear, her breasts level with my face, and I can't hear what she's saying with the music and the other voices so loud. At some point she gets dumped off Rob's lap and she's still talking to me, darting looks back and forth to the kitchen, and eventually I get up myself and leave her there and here's Dee Dee backed up against the stove, Robbie nodding at her as she talks and his right hand on her waist, thumb tracing a line up and down to her belly. Dee Dee watches me come in and she says, "I'm mad at you." She bursts into tears and runs out of the room. Robbie says, "She'll get over it." He gives a wink and goes back to the couch.

——

All over the goddamn world. That's what I think tonight: I've been working with the crew all day, finishing up what's left to get out of the fields, and I've explained how we're going to load it all up for transport. P.J., in particular, looks wary. He wipes the sweat off his face while I'm talking, staring straight at me. This is my last chance to do right by them and he doesn't believe it's going to happen.

It's still hard to know how I feel about losing this.

I could leave right now, and by the time I got to the airport it would be two in the morning, prime time for Saudi international departures. Somewhere up on the board would be where I would go. You leave or you stay. One time Cal and I were picking up supplies in Al-Kharj, which is basically a shithole—every can in the grocery's covered with dust, but we buy it anyway, and they have produce in the market stalls, even if it's not fresh and you're not sure what it is. We get bread. Cartons of bleach, cigarettes, and Kleenex tissues that we use for everything because they're cheaper and more abundant than toilet paper and they don't seem to have heard of actual napkins or paper towels. While we were waiting for the diesel to be fueled up a couple of Bedouin men walked by us, coarse brown robes trailing in the sand and wound over with ropes and ties, and Cal asked me, pointing, "How old do you think that one is?" The man's weathered face looked ancient to me, but Cal said, "No: he's probably thirty, if a day. You see that?" Cal said. "That's how you get, if you make it out here. That's what you want." Cal's forty-three and his complexion says sixty. I'm twenty-seven. Here, that isn't supposed to be young anymore.

—

Another day with the crew shooting me mutinous looks: they used to like me, more or less, and now I'm just another asshole. Why should they care if it's not my fault?

Nine o'clock at night and Cal's back, with a quarter of my month's pay from Sheikh Halim. I ask him where the rest of it is. He slaps his visor on the wall to get the sand loose and doesn't look at me. "You're getting yours," he says. "Better'n I can say for *them*." So the Sri Lankans are still screwed, and the Mexicans—all of us, basically, our whole little patchwork tribe out here in the dunes.

I shove a pile of dirty clothes off the easy chair and Cal sits down to roll a joint. The couch is the only place I spend any time, these days—it's just easier, I can stretch out and pile anything I need on the coffee table where I can reach it without getting up. I kick some more stuff off and try to ignore the shreds and stains of my living here. The copies of *Newsweek* on the floor must be over six months old. Last time I looked, Princess Diana had had another baby; then again, that would have been Dee Dee's turf, not mine.

"You know, I should be more pissed off than I am," I say.

"I would be," Cal says.

"You don't have to be."

"I've never had to be," he acknowledges. "There was that one time, though—ten years back when Halim thought he wanted to do chickens and then tried to cancel the whole game after I'd imported the fuckers and set everything up. No money, of course. I told him fine, but within half a day I could sell off the whole goddamn stock to the first passing Bedouin tribe so I'd get my money one way or another. Spooked the shit out of him, for some reason." He laughs and passes me the joint.

"Those chickens *smell bad*, Cal." It's his wife, Jaidee, who comes out from the kitchen. His third wife, to be exact: he met her on a business trip to Thailand. Her footsteps, in socked feet, are surprisingly loud for a woman her size. She's tiny and doll-like, the tails of one of Cal's blue-and-white striped shirts hanging down past her knees. You can just tell that she's pregnant, a bulge like a taut little cantaloupe brushing up against the cloth.

"Yeah honey, those chickens do smell bad," Cal says.

Jaidee ignores him, brandishing a container of salt in my direction. "How old," she demands.

I ask her where she found it. "Refrigerator," she says. "But it's sticky on the bottom."

"I have no idea," I tell her.

"Ha, well, *you* don't cook," she says, smiling.

"Honey, you want to make us some iced tea?" Cal says, passing the joint again.

"Oh yeah," Jaidee says. "*First* I clean, then I can make it for you."

"Shit," I say. "I'm sorry. You don't have to—"

"Well, okay," Cal says. Jaidee shakes her head at us like we're mentally deficient, and disappears behind the refrigerator that serves as the partition to the living room.

"You know," Cal says, "you could have knocked Dee Dee up."

"I believe her exact words on the subject were, 'fuck that noise,'" I say. We don't talk about it much. Cal said he was sorry, though, when she left, and once explained earnestly that if I wanted to stay and not go crazy, an Oriental woman might be the only reasonable thing to consider. It's either that or the occasional fuck with the expat girls, he said.

Which is Robbie's preferred route. I hear his truck pull up outside and there's a lull during which I hear muffled voices. Then he's pounding on the door.

I open it and he's holding a carton of bottles, not even wrapped up in clothes or stashed under food or anything. "Man, you didn't even cover this?" I ask in response to his shouted greeting. It's been a good three, four months since I've seen him last. Behind him are three women, one thirtyish and a British nurse, I'm guessing from the tone of her hellos, and the other two younger, probably Army brats from one of the compounds outside of Riyadh.

"Shit, Rob, you know that's not cool," Cal says. "Especially with them." He nods at the women, and the one who looks the youngest, a bubblegum-lipped little blonde thing, rolls her eyes.

"Aw, fuck it," Rob says. He puts the box on the card table by the refrigerator and smiles at the women while they remove their abayahs from over their jeans and T-shirts. They give us little waves and float into the kitchen to join Jaidee. "It's late, and anyway coming out from Palace Road some poor asshole hit a camel with his truck, it was backed up for fucking miles and we just went off-road past Al-Kharj all the way here. No one to see us."

Robbie also has a shitpile of cocaine, which he removes from his jacket pocket and then reconsiders when Cal tells him Jaidee's making Thai food, and we should all eat first before we get too fucked up. So we light another joint, and Robbie starts telling us about the latest goings-on at the new catfish farm where he's working now. "I was kicking ragheads out of the pools every day until we put the fish in," he says. "They think it's fucking bathwater, you know?" We're smoking and I'm starting to think the haze makes it look a little better in here, kinder and less in-your-face awful.

A little while later Jaidee's got the food out, good spicy stuff, and she sits on Cal's lap in the easy chair while they eat. Robbie's talking up the Brit and the other girl, who has sort of a pudgy face but major tits going on, which is the obvious attraction. By the time he starts talking about "the plan"—which by now has morphed into the idea of running his own septic business—the chubby girl is next to him on the arm of the couch, and Rob's hand is shoved right underneath one massive breast.

The British woman gives me a once-over but I beat hell out of range. I end up in the kitchen scraping out the bowl of peanut chicken and then the blonde comes in, asking for another drink.

"You are?" I ask. I splash grapefruit juice and grenadine in with the grain sidiqui to take the fire off.

"Kim," she says. She takes the glass from me while I mix another for myself. Now I think I can place her: the daughter of Colonel What's-his-name, the lifer on his third or fourth wife who can't keep his hands off each new crop of nurses and flight attendants who come through Saudi every year regular as swallows.

"And who are you," she says in a bored tone. No affected sigh: this one talks out of the side of her mouth for real.

"Todd."

"Really." She gives me a scorched-earth look.

We hear Robbie yelling, "Smells like money, baby," and the chubby girl squeals.

Kim leans against the counter and frowns. When Robbie shouts up again—this time, it's "Your shit is our bread and butter," which releases further appreciative squealing—Kim performs the exact same eye-roll she did earlier.

I consider that she's probably slept with Rob and doesn't want to get caught acting jealous. And she's cute, if laughable, when she swigs her drink like a pro and tamps down a cigarette before lighting it. Virginia Slims. She throws the lighter back down on the counter with overcalculated nonchalance and it skids off into the sink.

She laughs at this. "*Sorry*," she says.

"I think I've seen you before," I say.

"Yeah, party at Mike Diff's. Everyone saw me there."

Now I remember it. "Shit, that's right. Your father was in a bad way."

"Whatever." She shrugs. The T-shirt she's wearing is faded lilac, cut off over her tanned stomach. It says *Honolulu* in curlicue letters over her breasts. No bra.

"My dad takes me out to the desert a lot," she's saying. "We just hang out. You know. It's good to get away."

"Well this," I say, "*this*, Kim, is away. Very fucking far far away." I start laughing.

"Yeah," she says. "I suppose it is."

"Darlin', you have no idea."

She looks at me with a thoughtful expression, like she's deciding how maybe the night could go. I don't know.

"The fuck you are," Robbie shouts from the next room.

Jaidee and Cal come in and say that the girls are going over to Robbie's old trailer to set it up for the night. "No one's gonna want to sleep in here," Cal points out. Kim gives a little half-smile, mouth closed and one corner of her lip quirking up in a way that makes her look like she knows more than she should. "So I'll see you later," she says, going out with Jaidee. I hear everyone getting up and moving around, and the door opens so that the still desert night comes at us like a blanket. It swallows everyone up. Robbie lets the girls go first and says loudly that he'll be back to crash on the couch, but gives me a hammy wink as he says it. Cal pats Jaidee on the ass as she's leaving and then flips something to me from his back pocket.

"Here," he says. "Almost forgot. Picked it up from Halim."

It's my passport, wrinkled and creased, with the photo of me inside pouting like the pretty-boy jackass I was when I got here.

———

Yes like an animal, *no* like a man: I can look around the inside of my trailer and sometimes it's like walking into a mess that just happened, and I don't know when. You'd think I wouldn't be so disoriented. The way it's gotten anything wild could be penned up in here, plenty of crap and musk and god knows what else to root around in. It's all mine. Back in the first six months when I was waiting for Dee Dee to get here I know I kept it clean: sure it was a piece of shit, this place, but it was still going to be the first one that was just ours. I nailed down the carpet and pushed foam into the cracks around the windows and under the door to keep the sand out. Robbie and I took two days off to get into Riyadh and find a real mattress for the bed, an extravagant thing from Switzerland that cost a week's salary, but I knew she'd like it. "Yeow, honey!" she said when she saw it. "Get me down there right now. Let's start off our Little Shack in the Desert right." She was all pink from the heat, and dopey-eyed from days of traveling, but her hands were on my waist and down my pants like always, even better after so long apart.

And after that fast year, for a long time when I thought she'd still come back, I know I kept it up looking all right. I used the broom that she'd used and when Robbie and Cal were over dropping their ashes everywhere I pushed saucers at them to make it neat. Once Robbie said *wifey*, but Cal told him to shut up. "Just calling it like I see it," Robbie said. "What?" Cal managed to keep a straight face for a full minute before he said, lazily, "Well, Todd, you know—you have to admit, she *was* a great first wife."

That was the only time. A month or so later the divorce papers wended their way to me across continents and I fooled around with one of the city chicks who'd come out for a party, this nurse who'd made it over from some little town back in Michigan and whose way of posing her hand on her hip reminded me of Dee Dee, enough. "I just need to check in on what this is," she said the next morning. "Where are *we*, exactly?" I looked around the bedroom at anything but her and decided to let it all go to shit, the whole place, right then. *You don't ask that,* I thought. You either know what things are or you're just looking for what isn't there.

———

There's all that familiar rush of things, the movement of men and machinery, like the last part of a long journey. Crews go back and forth, pushing now that there's an end in sight. Efram and Manuel get the last field cleared; the stacks of wheat get loaded into trucks. Cal's crew drives the thirty miles to his place and then back. It doesn't let up.

At the canteen Bo's working nonstop. It's all the same, just more of it and all day, into the night. Grilled beef with canned jalapenos for the Mexicans, and with curry sauce for the Sri Lankans; french fries, as always. We've gone through twenty loaves of white bread in thirty-six hours. Robbie comes in around noon and starts swearing that unless someone drives out to the grocery in Al-Kharj to find some fruit or vegetables, his dysentery's going to kick in again and he hasn't got time to be shitting in the fields.

We sit out on the back steps and drink coffee. Robbie pops open a vial and does a quick line off the back of his hand. I figure I may as well.

"So what's up with what's-her-name, Ginny," I ask him. The fleshy girl.

Robbie snorts. "We're just having fun," he says.

"She informed of that fact?"

"I doubt she'll argue, you know?"

"Kim?"

He looks at me. "Why, you care?" I tell him no, just asking. He says she's a handful and gets too intense. "I mean, she's fucking nineteen. Been here since she was in grade school or something. She's a weird kind of lifer."

The girls are all still here, sticking mainly around Robbie's old trailer and spending time with Jaidee, doing god only knows what all day, I can't imagine. Who knows if they're even friends. Not that it matters; you make do. They can't leave until Robbie or someone drives them the three hours back to the city, which won't be until tomorrow at the earliest.

Of course, I've lost countless hours on my own, with nobody to help me do it.

"What's Halim paying you?" I ask Robbie. I'm sure he's been waiting for this.

"Enough," he says. "Cal told you. He wanted it done fast."

"He could have at least talked to me," I say.

"Well you shouldn't fucking have expected that. I hardly talk to him—Cal's got his ear, let him deal with it." He empties the rest of his coffee out into the sand.

I say, "He's trying to fuck me over. I've only got part of my money for the month, and he's been holding up the crew's pay longer than that. That's what *I've* had to deal with."

"Shit, Todd—it all gets worked out. Soon as everyone's moved over to Cal's, everyone gets paid. Don't fucking worry about it."

"It's a raw deal."

"Hey," he says. "Not my doing."

"Is that right?"

"Jesus." He stands and lights a cigarette, walking down the steps and stretching a bit. When we came over from the States we were both green, and we worked together all day assembling machinery from parts that didn't match and we had one truck between us to go anywhere and that first crew of Sri Lankans who'd never seen wheat. We threw dirt clods at camels to scare them off the freshly plowed ground while their Bedouin owners laughed at us. There was the sand in our tent until the trailers went up. You have to talk to someone when things are like that, and I think we did talk, then.

"You got money?" he asks me.

"Bank, yes. Ready cash, just a couple months' pay lying around."

"Well," he says.

"Are you telling me to use it?"

He's not looking at me, doesn't want to. Then he says, "Well, if it were me—" He gives a low whistle, shaking his head as he lights another one. For what seems like long minutes we listen to the belch of the trucks in the fields, smell the tang of gas in the hot sun. He wants me to say—what? That he's somehow responsible for the fact that I'm getting screwed over now? That he's dealing with life as it is here and I can't? Or that I think he tried to fuck my wife? How pointless it all seems, suddenly. Looking at him standing there, he's trying to pull off a rendition of Cal, the Early Years, or something else that I can't quite believe because it just doesn't convince me enough. It's like he wants to see if I'll just let this all go, lose it. What he knows he can't do is give the final push.

Finally he checks his watch. "Gotta get back out there or something'll be messed up," he says. I could be wrong, but he looks a bit ashamed.

"Check the diesel levels, will you?" I tell him. "We need enough for at least another day." He gives me a salute and goes back in the canteen.

I'm still thinking about this when night rolls around. Efram and his crew have departed, taking a slow caravan of combines and water trucks down the road to get them to the other farm. Heading back to the trailer I catch sight of P.J., walking with the other guys back to where the showers are set up behind their quarters. I wave, feeling like shit, and he gives me a look letting me know exactly what he thinks of my failure to pull through for them. It's no comfort to know that they're more indentured than I am.

I can hear everyone over at Robbie's trailer; the party's already in progress. Light comes out from the cracks around the frame, and the window—the one just like the canteen's—pulses with a weird glow. The thing looks like it was dropped out of the sky from somewhere. You can hear people stepping around, and Cal and Robbie's lower murmurs punctuated by the higher pitches of the women. Dee Dee used to come sit outside on our steps whenever the claustrophobia got to be too much; she said it was like being in a waiting room, only there was nowhere you were waiting to go.

It's like that now. I could stand here for a long time if I weren't so fucking tired.

When I get into my place Kim's lying on the couch, reading a paperback. Some spy-novel thriller, if it's anything she's picked up from the floor.

"Hey," she says. "I hope you don't mind. I needed to chill a bit."

"Not a problem," I say.

"Drink?" She shoves up and goes into the kitchen, which from my view is looking at least partially clean, probably Jaidee's efforts. Cal's place is spotless, every track and drip wiped away as soon as he makes it. Kim comes back out with cocktails in some kind of vase, which I recognize as part of a wedding gift Dee Dee always thought was ugly, and two glasses. Some of the drink slops out as Kim pours it. "It's my special recipe," she says, and seems embarrassed. "You add apple juice. It really cuts the sidiq." She hands me mine and waits for my reaction.

"Okay," I say.

"My dad taught me. He tried every kind of fruit juice—"

"It's fine."

I look at her watching me and she's a bit stung, I know it. Nineteen, Robbie said: right now she looks it, edges not yet there where she's trying to make them. Even though she's got that practiced aloofness in her eyes, her cheeks are still too soft and her face can't catch up when she tries to shift her stance to look less friendly.

She sits on the edge of the table and picks up a cigarette, tamping it down in a movement that already seems familiar. With the other hand she pulls her skirt out from where it's crept up underneath her thighs. The skirt's pink and stretchy. She lights up and blows smoke. She sizes me up: this time the look is part question, part challenge. We're both trying to figure out if there's anything to say.

Then we hear a truck horn blare outside. I can make out Robbie and Cal cursing and someone else trying to say something, maybe Jaidee, and Cal's yelling something back and she shuts up. I open the door as Cal lays on the horn again. He's pulling the truck around and Robbie's in the seat with him.

The air's balmy and it carries the stench of people packed together for too long. Cal revs the motor and sticks his head out the window. "Some fucking problem out by the worker quarters," he shouts. "Follow us."

"What?" I ask.

"I don't know. Some asshole kicked over a lantern or something and Bo says it's flaring up. Probably not a big deal, but it can't turn into a bigger one."

"Yeah," I say. They tear off and I see Jaidee standing outside, arms crossed, watching them go.

Kim's leaning on the table smoking, with an expression that looks oddly satisfied. When she asks what's the matter I tell her it looks like there might be a fire.

"Shit," she says. "Serious?"

"Hell if I know," I say.

I start looking for my keys. In the bedroom I fumble around on top of the dresser. More shirts, used tissues, riyal coins and a scattered row of little brass camels from one of our trips into the city long ago, to shop in the souks. That's the sum total of my collected cultural artifacts from this place. Nothing here seems to be worth anything. I sweep it all onto the floor and listen for a jingle —I've been on foot today, and I can't remember where I dropped the keys last night.

And now here's Kim at the door. "Looking for these?" she asks. She stands there like a stork, one foot resting up on the opposite calf, balancing like that as she dangles my key ring from two fingers. There's that little lopsided smile again. It's so appropriate I could cry. I come over and she drops the keys in my hand.

"Thanks," I say. I'm standing pretty close; for a minute we both hold our ground.

"Well," she says, smiling brightly. "Always business." She slides her foot down her very tan leg and swivels herself around, then out the door.

I go back to the dresser and rummage around in the top drawer, where I keep my socks. Underneath is the wad of bills stashed in there for expenditures. I count it quickly: several thousand riyals. I jam it all in my pocket. Now is the time to think. If I go anywhere, what else would I take?

Probably nothing.

In the living room Kim has moved back to the couch, and looks like she can't decide quite what she wants to do but she's making a big show of being back into her book. She's lying on her stomach with one knee bent, circling her foot in the air. When I tell her I'm going she says, "So maybe I'll see you later, maybe I won't."

The truck starts up and when I back away from the trailer there are two directions I can turn. One way puts me in Al-Kharj in under an hour, on a night like this: the summer moon is up and there's no haze, little wind, and you can see your way through the desert for as far as you'd want to go. There's that way and the money in my pocket and the shit I could leave behind for good. Then there's off down the road to the fields, where I see a glow. I can't tell how large the fire might be—the escarpments play a trick of perspective, jutting out and dwarfing everything we've built below. All I know is that way it's some fucking mess to deal with, something huge or maybe something puny and ridiculous, who knows till I get there, and after that I'm back here again and the only thing waiting is this place and these people and this girl. It's all I've got for right now. And she might be pretty—hell, some years off she'll likely be beautiful—but she isn't Dee Dee and she isn't my salvation and she can't be any kind of answer for very long. She isn't anyone.

SAFETY

Men

The oil man said that he'd heard I could hold my poison. Jane and I laughed at the corroded jumble of a still he'd brought back from the desert—we told him that we wouldn't drink the shit kind of hooch that was only good enough for rig roughnecks and Yemenis. "Hey, what d'ya want from me," he said. "Ask *her*," Jane said. She had her last ticket back to London in three weeks. Later, when we'd all switched to lemon gin and it was clear I wasn't going home that night, she said, "Watch it, darling. I wouldn't go for that one if I were you." I said I wasn't her and she just gave me her look, the one that means, you're a hard case, Kimberly.

He had money, coming off three years on a rig in the Empty Quarter. And he had that look men get here early, the weathering in a boyish face, gray flecks in the hair. He couldn't go back home, he said. Then they'd know how much he really had. But a nice life here in the city, settle down a bit, now maybe that wouldn't be so terrible . . . I was ready to be seduced again, for real.

We were at his place, an old villa with eight-foot walls around a garden and pool. If he'd bought a penthouse in the new Riyadh Towers, I told Jane, I'd just say forget it. Not waste my time with the nouveau.

"At this point?" Jane was giving up on me, and refused to collude.

"Everyone needs direction," I said. "He needs one."

"Look who's giving directions," she said, draping herself over the living room bar to light a cigarette.

The oil man found us there. "You women are all just so fucking gorgeous," he said. Jane slithered away but I let his arm rest on my hips.

Once I would have said to Jane: just stop me.

Shopping

On Tuesday I walked down in the al-Baatha Street souks, looking for a funnel. You cannot walk into a hardware store in Riyadh and ask for one. They know why we want them, and they don't want to sell them to us. I could have just taken the supplies from my father. But when he is out of the country my stepmother roams the house like a lost goat, flicking through fashion magazines and pacing between suntans and snacks, making me nervous. I make her nervous because she knows that she can do nothing to stop me when I find a way to go out.

If you know where to go like I do then you know that shopping between sundown and night prayers is the best time. Dusk blues the day's glare and what we wear doesn't stick. Head to feet, wrapped up in my black, and I'm ready to slip through the crowds like an eel. I left the driver on the main road that no longer smells of the open sewer that ran there fifteen years ago—the al-Baatha Street Yacht Club was the joke. I've got an old T-shirt somewhere to commemorate it. Now it's a wide marble median strip, throwing off glittery winks at the stall windows where gold hangs in ropes. And behind this shiny façade are the places we go when we can't get something through by Army post: lingerie or French perfume, which might be taken at customs, or birth control pills and Nitromin, which makes you wonder just who's really in charge here. And things like yeast, now banned from the supermarkets, and funnels and hoses, for distilling our sidiqui grain.

If I could tell Jane about it now I would say that of course I know you can't get caught. You pay attention. *Cover yourself*—this is no insult, when you know better; covering means hiding, and it's something to be good at, especially when you pique the interest of a red-bearded muttawein on the prowl for vice.

And when the stakes seem meaningless, you are good at hiding. Naturally, when the stakes were high, I slipped up.

Jail

Our day comes flicking in through the edges of a board over bars. The line of women, humped against the wall, stirs uncertainly as wood grates against metal and is shucked away. A piece of the sky is pale blue. Two of the black-clad shapes bob up, then squat again, whispering and ducking. Nothing happens. There's no shadow outside, only the faint slap of sandals on sand, retreating.

Manar rises and takes my hand. I don't know what time it is but it's later than when they came yesterday. I've slept. She leads me to the pool of light cast down through the bars and raises her arm in a graceful stretch, pulling her scarf from her head. When I do the same the new warmth is good. It's all right that it smells of gasoline, gutters, dust. Our cell is near the parking lot for the Friday mosque, where they used to pen camels when I was a girl.

The women get up and move behind us, gathering closer. Manar and I angle our faces to catch the rays; the other women inch nearer and lean up too. Everyone breathes in. Sand drifts over the sill and floats to the floor in front of us. I sneeze. Manar puts her arm around me and hums a mocking tune in my ear: "*Allahu, al'akbar* . . ." She makes me laugh, because we both know how mercy is dealt out here.

The women behind us leave their heads covered, save one who unwinds her veil and then opens her abayah wide in front of her, shaking her body out like a ratty bird drying its feathers. Her dress underneath is terrible: pink satin and cheap. She stares at us and shimmies again. Manar takes her time sweeping her gaze back to me, then tilts a refined jawline and says, low and precise in English, "prostitute."

Sunlight is a good diversion and it lasts for almost a full hour today. Then they replace the board, leaving just a few inches open at the bottom. Noon prayer starts up and the calls from the mosque outside waver in the air like transistor reception. Manar sighs: she is impatient. "Three days," she tells me. "This is really most unusual, even for him."

"Why do you think he did it?" I ask. Her charge is travelling without permission: her husband is on a business trip, and when she decided to take her driver and go to Jeddah the husband's older brother had her arrested.

"A stupid matter between brothers," she says. "Alim is older, he tries to order Talal about like a Paki. But Talal is smarter, he pays him no mind, so when he is away . . ." She takes a nail file from her leather sack and runs it idly over her fingers.

"Jeddah's over five hundred miles," I say.

"Yes, well?" Manar has a sly and lippy smile, glossed perfect red even after sleep. "I wanted to go shopping," she says vaguely. So we are both in trouble for shopping. Only she was after a new designer dress, and I bought a funnel and a hose for a man who turned out to be gutless. "Tough break," he said when I called him. That was that. My father is somewhere in Oman, Manar's husband is delayed in Dubai, and while we giggle together over our men the prostitute splays her legs out on the dirty concrete floor and picks at her teeth with her fingers.

Desert

My father took me out to the desert the day I turned nine-teen, four years ago. "Let's get the new truck dirty," he said. It was another white Toyota that looked exactly like the ones he'd been driving since 1975.

After that first summer when we moved here I went to the International School, less confused than most because there had never been autumn leaves back in California anyway at the time of year when I got new pencils and pens. I was mortified at my step-mother's desperate joy when the plaids and Shetlands arrived at long last from a catalogue. This was my first stepmother.

By nineteen I'd lost count of the trucks, and I was tired of toting up stepmothers. But that day going out to the desert I knew my father would let me drive once we passed the last wheat farm by the highway, where no one could see me behind the wheel.

My father told me, "Well, I'm going to give it one more go, Kimmy." I tried not to look too sorry for him at the prospect of trying for Number Three. We pulled off the road at the village past Al-Kharj. Midwess the tea man got up from his place in the shade to admire the new paint of the truck, already side-splashed with russety mud. I went to greet his wife Suha. Her little boys shrieked and spun around like tops, checkered ghotras winging from their heads. They laughed as they pulled on the wisps of light hair that slid down from under my veil. "'Salam," I told her. "My father gets married again."

"Inta?" Suha crossed her arms and waited for the news she al-ways wanted to hear. It was a joke with us.

"La." I shook my head. Not me, not yet.

In the dunes my father and I had dates and pumpkin seeds. "Never never again, *khalas*, I'm done!" I said. "I'm home for good." Tea from my thermos cup splashed out on the sand. I looked at the drops and studied the direction the wind was taking: it was shifting west. No, east. Maybe both spun together—the lip of the crest was at its mutable hour, looking for a map.

"Well." My father looked at me for a long time, as if trying to dredge something up. "If you stay," he said, "you'll need something to do." I had graduated from the Army high school in Madrid—just barely: I returned to Riyadh too often, leaving blanks in time served. They figured I'd done enough, in the end.

"I can always get another job."

"True," my father agreed. "That'll be good enough, for a while."

"Then there's after that," I said. At this he looked worried—or maybe resigned.

Midwess walked the edges of our little camp, listening for sounds above the wind. We'd staked up tents in case we decided to sleep out. My father and I took mouthfuls of seeds and spat them at the same time to see what pattern they'd make. It was a game the Bedouin children played, to determine the future. You ask a question and then read where to go based on how the seeds fall. My seeds flew out and then back and so did my father's. "Home free," he said, and we laughed.

The little boys begged to know what I wanted, but Suha quieted them: what was asked was a secret. My father knew that I thought I had my answer—"Try again, Kim," he urged—but I said no, I knew where I was.

"Four years for Ginny," I predicted, wanting to be optimistic. That would be a record, more than stepmothers One and Two, who hung on for ten months and three years respectively. We made fun of Number One for a few minutes—the one who'd said she was eager for adventure. "A pathetic sight, my eight-year-old daughter leading my crying wife out of the supermarket," my father said. That was when she learned that because there was a Coke factory in Israel, she'd only be able to buy Pepsi in Saudi.

"Well, it wasn't *exactly* the last straw," I said. I was trying to be at least a little bit encouraging.

No babies had come along to relieve their monotony. My father always said he tried, but I must have been some miracle of a peak sperm count and that was it for him. We no longer discussed my real mother. A childish twenty when she had me, she was gone by the time I was four, waving away her claims with the assertion that she had other things to find out about herself.

My father and I made merry bets that day. "Let's see—Bob Alexander, Jeff McDonald, McDaniel, or that new Swedish guy over at Vinnell—what's his name?"

"I don't think so, Dad."

"It'll have to be somebody at some point. We'll have to marry you off."

I laughed. That day, we had no need to be serious.

"I've got time," I said.

"Kimmy—" he started to say, and then Suha whistled, two quick high notes, and we looked behind us. Fifty feet away a wolfish desert dog snapped at a plastic bag that had drifted from the rug where we sat. One shot from Midwess's rifle caught the dog clean in the skull.

The boys cheered, sending shrill whoops into the air. Suha looked anxious but my father's expression did not change. A minute passed and then he said, "Happy birthday."

Home

This is the place I know, and it sticks to you, filmy, fluid as the sand that eats at the edges of anything they build up. I've hardly ever left. Away I am made nervous, by streets and sidewalks, Walk Don't Walk, trains, and lines of bodies shouting for tickets, for places and items, ribbon lanes speeding into their own hems. Or alien scents, like skunk on a back road; idiot dogs bounding from yards and cars, pissing and wagging, immune from the crack of a gun.

"You have to go somewhere when they make you leave," Jane said once. "Be an expat in London if you can't handle the States. Or anywhere." She assumed that I'd know how. I am a dependent of my father, a *dependent of a person*, says my official passport for Saudi Arabia, which I've had for so long that my other one, blue and bland and American, isn't anyone I know. When they say you're too old to remain a daughter, you must go. Or, become something else.

Jail

Thirteen is unlucky, I tell Manar. See? There are thirteen of us here. Not good.

"It's the Kuwaitis who are unlucky, not us," she says. We sit on her rug, leaning into the choice corner farthest from the low arch in the wall that leads to the toilet. Manar donated a sheet to tack up over the opening so that we can squat in private. That's why we have this corner.

I've heard that expectant mothers keep a packed suitcase at the ready for when their water breaks. Manar says, same here—and if you're smart, you have one packed up for any sudden excursions to prison as well. Hers is a red leather Mark Cross.

I take the newspaper that her sister folded into her box today. When we lined up in the visitors' room this morning I heard Manar say to her, leaning close to the screen: next time bring the *Gazette*, too, for her to read. They touched their foreheads together through the mesh before parting—not their lips, as the other women do.

These other women are practically invisible to Manar, like flies, though they irritate her when they grow uncontrollable and loud, weeping for news of money raised for their release.

"In two days Talal will be back," Manar says. "Then I am out. My sister says we will have a plan." She gives me a sudden look that might be mistrust. Then she smiles again and resettles her face. We unpack her box: food in containers, which she will share with me; a dress, another pillow, magazines, tight cotton gloves that she will put on after smoothing cream on her hands—Chanel Cristalle. Not No. 5; it is too old for her yet, she says.

Before I open my box I look to see what the other women have. Many have received nothing: their relatives are too poor to come every day. They hoard their stale pita bread and drink the water brought round in the afternoon—water Manar and I don't have to touch, drinking from our purified stash. Someone has told my stepmother to put bottled water in with my food. Like the relatives of some of these women, my stepmother is afraid to come to the jail, or ashamed. Whatever the case her presence would be pointless. Mujdi the houseboy handed over my box, saying to me, "Inshallah, inshallah—you come home," with grave eyes.

Two big bottles of water today. Bananas, and crackers and peanut butter: my stepmother must have gone to the Army commissary. Sandwiches, too. "Look at this," I say to Manar. "It's ham." Manar laughs, taking the offending item. She pokes at the forbidden meat, tastes the mayonnaise and makes a delicate pinched face of dislike. "Is she stupid?" she asks. I will have to eat it: the guards gave our boxes a cursory check today, but they might look through the trash later, you never know.

While I chew I think of the waste. My stepmother lives for our monthly rations of ham, pork chops, and bacon; when my father and I are on our own, we barter or sell it to the other expats. That she is sharing it with me is a gesture I can only interpret as a hostile act—although then I would have to credit her with intelligence, more than I'd like to.

Manar leafs through the latest British *Vogue*, not bothering to shield it from the other women, whom she assumes cannot read. She goes fast enough to inflict violence on the pages. Soon she appears bored and takes a photograph from her purse. I bend closer to see three dark-eyed girls, sitting together by a courtyard fountain, a wash of long silky dresses in emerald, gold, sapphire blue. "My daughters," Manar says.

"They're lovely." I hold the picture and see that one of the girls, the tallest of the three, has not bothered to hide the Nikes on her feet under the pouf of shiny fabric. The house behind the girls has a corridor and arches inlaid with gleaming tiles—the new kind, made to look traditional.

Manar taps her fingers on the magazine, looking at me. Then she smiles. "I know," she says, reaching for her vanity case. She rims my eyes with kohl—a light touch only, she says—and paints intricate henna vines spiraling down through my fingers. We're aware of the other women watching us. The prostitute's hands are thickly smudged; she would be obvious from twenty paces. Manar is deft and subtle for me. When she's finished she stands and holds up a mirror. There is the deep smudge around blue, the prettiness of red on my wrists. It is a contrast like certain flavors that conflict on the tongue.

Later the light changes. When it grows too dim to read Manar and I cover our hair again and lean back to the wall, closing our eyes, and become one shadow with my face the only alien color in the room.

City

Somewhere down the hall, the two Abdullahs were arguing. Their excited voices pitched out the conference room door and made their way into my inner sanctum. I was in a little room tucked behind Walid's office. To get in, I opened a closet door and pushed aside a clutch of mops and broomsticks and slid through another hidden door. It wasn't likely that any patrolling muttawein would bother to investigate this far.

What had my father been worried about? I'd only needed to *say* that I knew how to type. Once or twice a week, maybe I did, or I sent a telex to Walid's home office in Beirut. Riyadh was growing fast: our firm had a lot of work. But for me it was all really about tea, endless sugary glasses of it that I drank with the Saudi clients. These conversations often concluded with an invitation to spend time on a yacht in Marbella. There were so many boats.

I was twenty-two.

I sat there smoking. The office boy had brought my dinner and a fresh pack of Dunhills, and Walid probably wasn't coming back after evening prayer.

With nothing to do, I punched an extension on the phone to see if Sean was still in the building. He picked up and I said, "Get me out of here."

"Knocking off already?" he joked. Sean was amiable: the kind I was pulled toward then, a middle ground.

"Two minutes."

I tossed on my abayah and wrestled with my large shoulder bag—various changes of clothes, makeup, a hair dryer, two books (just then it was *Fear and Loathing in Las Vegas* and *Far From the Madding Crowd*), birth control pills, a water bottle. These were the essentials.

Out of the office we lit more cigarettes. It was a balmy night, city smells gone fecund in the midsummer heat. And even sand smells like raw dirt when it's being dug up. 1988: Riyadh was being paved over with new high-rise buildings and malls. It retained its older ghost-image in my head.

"How's your dad?" Sean asked in the car.

"Not so good." As I'd predicted, Ginny was threatening decampment. She'd gone on a long holiday back to Richmond or wherever it was she came from, and it wasn't clear whether she'd be back.

Past the new souks—storefronts decorated to look like old-time merchants' stalls—we turned off an overpass onto an unfinished highway access road. Bedouin men crouched around a television set they'd rigged up to the cigarette lighter in a truck. Nearby, in a dusty lot, camels were tied to bumpers and a few women sat together in the truck beds, laughing at a high-decibel game of tag played by the children. Odd moments of quiet came in between the thrum of cars overhead. I made Sean stop to buy Vimtos from an old woman selling them from a washtub. The sodas were like Coke with extra sugar, with a tang of pomegranate.

We went to a party. I jiggled my tequila sunrise, which was actually a cocktail of sidiqui tempered with grapefruit juice and slimy wedges of blood orange. "The same old shite," Jane said, when she found me. I told her no, the orange was new. The host was just back from Spain. "Someone is always just back from Spain, darling," she said.

Jane's father was a British neurologist, and she was a fairly recent friend of mine. She had a nursing degree and I had my job at Walid's. We thought we were getting old. She was looking for someone who would leave; I was looking for someone who wouldn't.

We'd dated brothers, married men, college boys over for a summer, our father's friends. The sad ones, we agreed, were the ones who couldn't leave if they wanted to. They came to the parties too, standing together in their outdated patterned shirts with too-wide collars: the beta males. We knew them all. Leo with the failing air-conditioning business, Roger who was getting ripped off by the Korean cooks at the taco restaurant nobody wanted to go to. There was a saying: quick money and get out, or get a Thai wife. That's the direction they were going.

"Kiss kiss," Jane trilled as her father walked up to us. He was wearing a funny hat, like a pilgrim's, black with a buckle; it was just after the Fourth of July.

"Sweetheart," he said to me, "you should have a look in on your pops."

"You should have a look at yourself, Daddy," Jane said. He was still in his white coat from the hospital, and the contrast against his florid face wasn't anything we hadn't seen before.

He laughed this off and headed to the bar for a refill, waving his hand in the direction of the back bedroom. "Oh, leave it for once," Jane said. She tugged on her fishnets, which were beginning to relax into the heels of her spiked pumps. I was sporting my high-summer look of all white, to show against tan and gold. "Tell me about Sean," she said. "What's happening there?"

Nothing much was happening there, but I saw Jane following his progress across the room. He was talking to a young compound brat in a pink tube top, though he didn't look like he was taking her seriously.

"Sean," I said, "is a distinct possibility."

"Oh," Jane said. She snapped her eyes off him.

I found my father in the back hallway, leaning against a Grecian pillar that made no sense in the expat-souk scheme of décor. Two British nurses were on either side of him, and he veered precariously to the left and then to the right as he tried to keep talking to both. "This is the colonel," one of them said, pushing her hand at his shoulder where the stripes and pins were. She persisted in saying this while the other woman giggled. "Now how'd those get there?" he said.

"Hey, Dad."

"Kimmy!" He lifted his drink in a salute. I could tell he'd been going at it for some hours.

"*It's the daughter*," one nurse whispered loudly to her friend.

It had been a few days since I'd been home—maybe more. My father knew I could take care of myself. By then, to tell the truth, we both held top slots on the Star Map of legends in town. But that night he just looked tired. He couldn't figure out how to stop living up to his billing even if he'd wanted to.

"*You're having me on Bonnie?*" Now they were conducting their conversation behind their hands, as if that muffled anything.

"*He's married, I told you—*"

"*Did I say I cared?*"

They went on furiously, each still staking her claim. My father shrugged and gave me his familiar rueful grin. I asked him how things had been going lately.

"Malish," he said. Whatever. "You know. Up to no good in the city that always prays."

Hail and Farewell

They all blur together. Arriving every July, after their schools let out and they'd made their goodbyes, and there they were suddenly at the pool or in the game room on the compound, stranded without the cars or friends they'd had. They'd had adventures on the way over—maybe in Athens, maybe Munich or Madrid—and now they were riled up. The remaining half-summer loomed without prospect. They presented what they knew best of themselves: a reputation for getting kicked out of boarding schools, or sunny cheerleading pictures, a clutch of trophies to put on a shelf. They holed up in posses, sneaking drinks from their parents' cabinets and playing cassette tapes they bought in the souks. They watched videos of MTV. One girl watched *The Thorn Birds*, over and over, and gave haircuts for ten dollars; another did Jane Fonda workouts at the gym, going for the burn. The girls disdained the wives and sauntered around the compound in the skimpy clothes they couldn't wear when their fathers made them dress up for Army dinners or a trip to the Intercontinental Hotel for brunch. The boys began to disappear: either off to college or anywhere they could work, because in Riyadh no work meant no car, no money, and no way to have sex. Or they disappeared indoors, sulking, once and a while emerging to sit on the front steps of their identical houses and smoke cigarettes in the heat, defeated into basic existence.

Or they tried to stay, but it was usually too late. They had other lives waiting. One girl, from California like me, got a job in one of the Army mail rooms. Every morning we boarded the van with the other women who worked in the city; we left at six-thirty and the driver made five stops before we were all let off. This girl seemed like she might stick around. This was 1982: she said she was having more fun than she'd thought, once I started taking her out. She even dated Sean for awhile—back then he was too new for me, too green. I left for Madrid for my last year in school and she and I made plans for a backpacking trip the next summer, Italy and Greece maybe, and then we'd just see. Her last letter was from Los Angeles: "Hey, I got UCLA," it said. There were a lot of exclamation points after that.

Jail

"Where is your father?" Manar asks. I've told her that he's in Oman, but that's not what she means. She wants to know why he hasn't sent me something specific, instructions, an order for what I should do.

"It's the government," I tell her. Paperwork. Red tape. At my age he can't argue to keep me in the country, supervise me—four months until my twenty-fourth birthday, they'll say: the legal limit. Deportation is the only thing that can be in the works.

Manar has also had news today, and it's making her restless. Talal has been delayed.

We are twelve now: the Filipino maid has been retrieved by her Saudi employer. Who knows why she was left here so long? Perhaps she was being punished for some infraction, or perhaps she was simply forgotten. When she was called by the guard, she gathered her bundle and went out with her head down, her expression more fearful than when she was brought in.

Manar and I have had a bath today. This morning her sister brought a carton of Evian water, more than we could drink in a week. It was still cool from a refrigerator. After some words with the guards—and an exchange of money—we were permitted half an hour in a small room where we stripped down and sat on a bench, pouring water from the bottles over our heads and down our backs. Now we're perfumed. Our hair is still damp and we sit like queens in our corner again. I've discarded my dress, an old cotton-print for the souks, and Manar has given me one of hers.

Incense pots smoke at our feet, keeping the cockroaches at bay. The guards don't usually look at Manar and me—the prisoners of privilege, the ones they know will offer up the biggest fine—but now it is day five here for both of us, and when the sharp-faced younger guard brings food for the others he sends us a warning glance with his eyes. We are taking up space. Our men have not co-operated as quickly as was expected.

Wives

My stepmother opens the curtains at eight in the morning, flips the shades to get the dust off that silts through the cracks of the window frame during the night. She clips marigolds from the pot and sets them on the table, so that any neighbor can see them from the path outside. Then she goes back to bed. When Mujdi comes at eleven she lets him in to sweep and vacuum; when he leaves, she has a drink. There will be tea with the wives later. And the pool. Maybe in the evening, she will pull an abayah on over a long dress and join the women on the bus to the grocery store, or go shopping in the souks downtown, short blocks from where I wait and breathe. She must do these things or she'll go crazy.

Nomads

In Athens I sat with him at a long table under olive trees, drinking retsina as the sun went down. I had not been in the mood for bitter wine but when he said, "Don't sit there with me with nothing," I went ahead and ordered it. His year was over and he had money, so I got the most expensive stuff on the menu.

"Here's to Al-Farad Aluminum," he said. "I still can't believe those fucking idiots. I won't see that kind of dough again for years."

"That's true," I said, and I didn't add that he would have had much more if he'd stayed on because we'd had that conversation already. He spoke of what he'd do after, other years elsewhere.

Or at the restaurant on the island with windmills behind us, where he refused to touch the octopus on my plate because, he said, he was out of that godforsaken place now and could make them bring him a steak. When the waiter put the meat on the table a harbor dog squatted five feet away, lifted its tail and shat an endless stream.

Cyprus, Gibraltar, Corfu: we only went places with sun.

"Come visit," they said, back to Texas, Dublin, Atlanta.

I was eighteen, I was twenty, then twenty-three. When he was over as the others had been over I looked right through him and it was as if he'd never lived, as if there wasn't even death to keep walking toward.

In Athens, he took my hand under the table. But they all did that.

Jane and I took our last trip together before her final weeks in Riyadh, before I met the oil man. She wanted one last fling and she flashed her diamond around to get it. I asked her why she hadn't left it at home. "With my father?" she said. "Are you kidding?" Not that the ring was a problem, and her fiancé in London would never know. We were giddy at the airport while we waited; we smoked, and fidgeted with magazines, and Jane flicked contemptuously at her abayah and said, "I can't wait to get *this* off." When the pilot announced we'd left Saudi airspace, we piled them under our seats.

And at the halfway mark on the flight back, we swathed ourselves again, burned shoulders sliding under black fabric. Jane was careful to not let anything show.

Jail

Tonight even the board across the window can't hide the moon. Instead of sleeping, Manar and I have laid our heads quietly against the wall, watching the light seep in.

"I wonder," she says in a whisper. "Did you think he would marry you?"

The oil man or someone else, I tell her. It wasn't a matter of love——just a way to buy time. Settle in, get something of my own; a stake in the future where the rest could be worked out later. "It's no different than my father and the women he marries," I say. The darkness is making me bold.

"They think there is a thing they can change in him," says Manar.

"Except they don't know the first thing."

"But you." She's studying me, her smile heightened in the strange muted glow of the room. Across from us someone stirs and coughs.

We curve in closer, knees touching through black silk.

I tell her I have nowhere I want to go. I tell her that Ginny is my father's fourth wife and that she won't last either; her trips to the States get longer and longer. "And now, if there's war," I say. "He'll never leave."

Manar says, "Of course, there are always other ways . . ."

"Such as."

"Solutions that are more interesting," she says. "You for instance."

Now we are playing a game. She does love Talal now, she says. You understand, she says, that it came to be this way. I say I understand. She says that what you can control is important. Talal would agree.

We shift in again, for another move. "Alim is the head of the family," she says. "He wants Talal to take another wife." It's why she's here—the reason she ran, the statement she made. The women in her family are trying to devise a solution. Her sister, her mother-in-law: they're on her side. "We all hate Alim," she says.

"But what can you do?"

"Sometimes," she says, "you can win on a technicality. And a mother always chooses a wife for her son."

The flame in the incense pot glows, and I watch a thin finger of smoke wind slowly up into the air where the light catches and holds it.

Manar knows how to twist the way things are done.

I say I understand.

The smoke encircles us, keeps our barrier, winds through our hair. I think of the shadowed faces of the others, the ones who will leave here alone.

Ein-Fadr

My father and I crouched over the platter of rice and meat while coffee bubbled up in a brass pot. The desert night was as clear as we'd ever seen it. It was the celebration after the long Ramadan fast.

There were tents, staked in a circle and garlanded with colored lights; a huge fire roared up in the center. Midwess walked from group to group, his extended family members and many friends. He was pleased to be the host of such a large gathering. The whole of his village had turned out for it. The men got into animated discussions while the women tried to keep the children in line and out of the fire, which they ran around and threw things into. Nobody could really keep still: food was passed back and forth, plates brought out with something new to try. People kissed and greeted one another as if they hadn't met in years. Suha made many trips past the tents to refill water pitchers from the large plastic jerry cans in the back of Midwess's truck.

My father and I had brought a friend of his along, an engineer from Georgia who spoke Arabic with a drawl. A shout of laughter went up when the sheep's eyeball was handed to him on a paper plate.

That night was in the spirit of friendship, but it was also a mark pointing out. When the sword dances began my father joined the men. The beat of the drums went on until late. The women clapped and trilled; they whipped their hair around and around, black raven wings flying out to make shapes in the glow of the firelight. Later, Midwess inquired as to the intentions of my father's friend, who in his confusion took him too seriously and in the process of stammering out a reply managed to insult me. So Midwess offered camels. If Suha was willing, he said gallantly, he would have no problem doing my father the honor of taking me off his hands.

When my father hedged, there was a goat or two thrown into the bargain.

Soon they were all laughing. Suha and I did too, but her expression was thoughtful.

"Not *yet*," my father said, bowing to his friend.

Suha asked me, in her careful English, "Some day?"

We sat together in the lee of the family's tent, letting the wind cool us. I wore a dress like hers: loose cotton with embroidery, the color of ripe grapes.

"Ayawah," I said. Yes. Still I thought: I didn't *have* to. Wasn't that the difference?

The fire flickered down and the stars took over for our light.

I will, I shall, *Inshallah*, I do.

Safety

Manar says that if there is war, it will be good. We are shored up against other changes, the ones that could break us. Here is a collusion: she is playing a trick, she will remain in the position she wishes to keep, and I am becoming that something else—dependent still, but of another kind, perhaps the only kind I can be.

Oh, Jane, I think. You'd never believe this.

But she's already gone too.

I pack up my things in the cell and wait for our fines to be paid. This is arranged by the mother-in-law, a stately dark beauty who assessed me yesterday morning when Manar presented me to her in the visitors' room. It didn't take long. I must look more temporary than I feel.

Which is good, I think. This is my game too, and who shows her hand all at once?

Or knows it?

"Alim will be up in arms," Manar says. This delights her. "And he can do *nothing*, because Talal is technically keeping his promise."

I will send word to my father: the call will come from me. Then the men will meet and talk.

The prostitute has gone this morning as well. As Manar and I stacked up our reading material and folded our clothes, she was called out. She took a long look at me as she went. After a week in that satin dress the pink was streaked with sweat and grime. We don't know who paid for her, but Manar suspects it was one of her cohorts who finally raised the money. "Who knows how they manage it," she says, and she pauses for a moment, concern on her brow. Then the look vanishes from her face.

So I am out in the city, out on the edge in the air. Manar's driver is coming for us and I look at her, her lovely profile triumphant, as she scans the street. She does not look at me. The sand lifts up in the wind like a cloth. Across from the mosque the car horns blare and vendors jostle carts and a truck careens around a corner, skidding into the median and then picking up speed again.

Down the street there's the shriek of brakes. Sounds gather together and are overlaid with others. It's past noon prayer; grates rattle up and voices are raised again, sun hits the windows and tosses off blinding glare, everything's shimmering and you can just see the new over-pass in the distance, where a caravan of water trucks pulses slowly like a mirage. I blink and they disappear. Back on the street it's hot and the men in white and the women in black lean for the store-front canopies where there is shade. I look at everything I know.

RUB AL-KHALI

"Say what you think," he says. "Should I get a divorce?"

I should tell my son something definite. Instead I talk about what he already knows: about the children. If his sons want a surfboard because they've been to California, is there any harm in it? They are good boys, I say. I tell him that their mother wants to show them the ocean just as she shows them the desert. "You are both doing your best."

"It isn't good enough anymore," my son says. He sounds almost violent, although he never is. Whiskey splatters from his glass.

Next door my neighbor raises the volume on the television and we hear the broadcast for sundown prayers. Outside the call echoes from the mosques—I have left the sliding door open. From twenty stories up the sound is thin.

"She couldn't bear to lose the children," Talal continues, "but I don't know if I could take them."

He means that he would not feel good about it. It is his right to keep the children, but I love him for being conflicted about it. I suggest they could work something out. Is there any need for a divorce? Maybe Kimberly just needs some time. At this Talal looks pained; then he stares down at his lap, where splashes from the two drinks he's had have decorated the front of his white thobe. I don't say anything about it. Lately, as he comes to talk with me more and more, we have the understanding that he will sleep on the couch once he gets past three, and it is clear he is headed in that direction tonight.

My son has a very big problem, but he does not really understand what it is. It has gone far beyond his comprehension. He has four daughters, two sons, and two wives. I would say that they have been happy—yes, all of them, at one time or another, if not now. And I know myself that these arrangements require constant maneuverings. When I look at Talal, I love him—my son, frowning now, shutting his eyes against the rising crescendo of the mu'addin pulsing through the walls—but what I also think is, *pitiful*.

"I'm disillusioned," he says. When I smile at him he almost laughs; it is an old refrain.

"Talal, you're going to have to get used to this. Now is when things will begin to change, and you must keep up with them." I move to the kitchen to find something for him to eat. "The girls are going to start in on you any day now."

"Leena wants to go to Switzerland," Talal says. "To Manar's old school. I should probably let her."

"Of course. You should."

But he looks firm for a moment—uncharacteristic. This is his problem. He has trouble forming his own resolve; he is beleaguered by the opinions of others. Changes worry him and then he becomes cornered and stuck. Absently he balls the rice I put in front of him, rolling it in his fingers but not eating it.

I think, don't pretend you can stop this.

"If Leena goes, she'll be speaking French in a year. You can buy her skis, and she'll lie to you about how many boyfriends she has. Or maybe she won't. She'll say, Daddy, I need to go to London next summer. Those big eyes of hers are only going to get more charming. Her sisters will be jealous. When you pop in for surprise visits she'll swarm you with her pretty friends, and you'll buy them anything they want in Geneva."

"Oh, I know," he laughs, loving this idea of his eldest. "Spitting image."

"No, Manar was never like that," I say. "You only thought so."

"Probably," he says, and we don't talk more about either of his wives.

———

Talal is asleep. I slide the door open and take a glass of tea out to the balcony. At sunset the desert edges into the city: the sand is melon-tinged, and rays spill over roofs and water towers and bright blue swimming pools. Riyadh is beautiful like this. It is impossible for me to say how happy I am here.

Sitting, watching, I feel young.

It is my daughters-in-law, not my sons, who do not understand why I live in the towers. *So modern*, Kimberly has said. She remembers when they were built, after she came here as a girl, and a district of market stalls was obliterated. Of course, having the luxury, she imagines it a tragedy of progress. For Manar the objection is one of space—she needs more to make her presence felt and is always redecorating the girls' rooms or the big hexagon space off the kitchen where the women gather, or Talal's study. In my five rooms, she sees a condition of reduced circumstances.

But my circumstances are not reduced. Here, in fact—here in this high gleaming tower, which throws its glare from the windows like a beacon—here there are worlds wound together with years. Like the balcony below mine, where skinny palms, their roots trapped in brass pots, nevertheless reach their fronds up to brush past the edges of the cement rectangle where I sit. It is a tiny oasis in the sky. Or two across and one up, the old man who naps outside on a rug each afternoon with his goat. The family in the penthouse increases each year; the wife swishes briskly through the lobby with glittering abayahs tossed over her smart pantsuits, and she is trailed by a retinue of Filipino nannies who manage the growing brood with cell phones and date books and drivers. There is space enough for visitors, if we want them—but also a containment, if we do not. The towers are efficient. When I look over the city I can see what is beyond—for the desert is never far—and when I move about my rooms they are spare and orderly, each thing in its place, as I once made my things so in a tent. And sometimes, like now, with the last ring of prayer fading away, it is quiet. This is what I am reduced to, and it opens wide.

———

Manar sips at her champagne, which is the kind from the market, fancy bubbling grape juice and not one drop of alcohol. In front of the girls she doesn't like them to know that I would usually drink the other kind.

"It's too *sweet*," her youngest lisps. She should not be so coy at four.

"Go play in Grandma's bedroom," Manar says.

The girl sticks her fingers in her mouth and runs off to join her two sisters. They're still content to play with dolls; this year's favored model is a ballerina, cream-skinned and tutued. Also, English and expensive.

Manar herself looks expensive, though she is always tastefully so, just the right amount of Dior here or Chanel there. And she is thriftier than an untrained eye would know. Talal's architectural firm is prosperous, but Manar has had to learn an economy—of a kind.

"Well," she says, "you managed to convince Talal."

She is hiding a sulk.

I want to ask her, whatever happened to your brain?

She has brought a maid with her to serve us lunch—this is the usual pattern for the weekly visits with the girls. Manar needs to believe she is generous. With her own mother she would not dare; that woman is forthright with her control, which encompasses her daughter but does not extend to Talal. Whereas I am seen to have influence with decisions my son will make. This is true—we both know he is pliant, but since Kimberly came he has had two directions to go, and Manar played her own part in that.

Now she provides her offerings and thinks that I might bend her way once more.

The maid brings a tray of sweets. Manar chooses a button-sized pastry and says, "But of course, I want to thank you." She arranges herself straighter in her chair; she will not lounge. "However there is . . . well, you see—" Now she looks distinctly uncomfortable.

I wait: whatever it is, I will learn how she has not quite had her way in the matter.

"It's just that—well, you know that Leena is not veiled yet. It's worrying me no end. I'm sure—"

"Manar," I tell her, "this is normal. Leena has just turned fourteen; she's perhaps a little late, but there's nothing to worry about. I was nearly fourteen when I started." This is not true, exactly; I managed to hide evidence of my monthly flows for six months. When I admit this Manar's mouth falls open in surprise. "But why—would you?" she asks.

"Don't be delicate," I reply. Her attitude is maddening and I do not understand it: she has had every advantage. "Of course," I continue, "we were just desert girls."

"I didn't mean—"

"Of course you did not."

"I was thinking," she asserts herself, "perhaps just to wait one more year. That she would be better suited, afterward." I raise my eyebrows, and she looks distressed. "Why would any woman—" I begin.

"Yes, *Umma*, thank you!" Our object of discussion comes from the bedroom, smiling, and drops to the floor by the coffee table. There is an awkward silence while we wonder how much Leena has heard.

"It's nothing," I say. "Your father is happy for you."

"Well, but I *appreciate* it. You know—sometimes he gets . . ." She looks sidelong at her mother and stops. Leena reaches to the tray for a cookie, and her smile becomes falsely demure. She can be swift like this in her little manipulations; Manar remains composed, though she is rigid and her features pinch inward. Leena crosses and uncrosses her legs, wipes sugar on her jeans, and checks the time on her watch, which is large and pink and plastic. She fiddles with the gold bangle on her other wrist and then changes it to the same arm as the watch.

I find bits of her around the apartment for days after she comes: magazines, a bottle of ruby nail polish, lip balm and coins shaken out of her purse, which now lies abandoned on the kitchen counter. Little things fallen from anything she's picked up or moved and put down again. "Mama got these for me," she'll say, holding out new earrings or combs which will end up in the cushions of the sofa. Every object part of an act she does not know she is playing, the things that could break wide-open once she is gone.

Now she says to her mother, "They're napping," tossing her head in the direction of the bedroom. Manar nods, tracing the contours of gold on her own wrist, and we all smile politely from three separate spaces facing in.

—

With my grandsons there can be chaos—it depends on where we are. Today it is the park, and as I sit on a bench with Kimberly and watch them I can sense her internal calculation of how far it might go.

There did not used to be grass here. Or anywhere, in the city: our gardens were palms or vines, but in recent years we have become wasteful. At least this is how I think of it—water still being, to me, a thing you are grateful for and do not throw away. Now we have blades plump and lush like a showy green carpet, and fountains that gurgle up rain. My grandsons splash and shriek. Away from the spray, little girls sit together and pull all the clothes off their dolls.

"I can't think of what else to do," Kimberly is saying. "You don't have to tell me that I'm still mucking around in limbo, Thurayya." I smile: but for my American daughter-in-law, my given name is no longer on anyone's lips.

"It's all right if you want to go home for awhile," I tell her. "You know that's the trouble—that you never did."

"I guess," she says. She sighs and adjusts her abayah over her dress. At the concrete table next to us are young mothers, such as we produce these days: high-heeled feet swinging out from the edges of black silk, gym-toned calves peeking from khaki capris. There are no men in the park, so their veils flip casually from their hair in the breeze. "They could almost be in Connecticut," Kimberly says, though since she has never been there herself she sounds less than certain. The mothers ignore their children and nannies and take speculative glances at Kimberly in between sips from their Starbucks cups. They can see that Ahmed and his brother have reddish glints in their hair; they can see that Kimberly's dress is gauzy and old-fashioned, though they cannot fault her abayah, which is whispery and light like theirs. They can hear us speaking English, and they know exactly what she is. But they also see me, so they keep their voices low.

Horns blare behind our bench where traffic snarls on the avenue. A long Cadillac drives up onto the sidewalk. The teenaged boys packed inside cheer as they urge the driver on, running over a bush before pulling close to a car loaded with girls. In a rapid-fire exchange, balls of paper sail through the windows. A quick flash of eyes and mouths and the girls are gone—the boys whip out their cell phones and start dialing.

Ahmed runs up to us and asks if he can go to the monkey bars. A little band of boys waits for him there with the nannies milling around them; they are inking words on paper and taping them to the boys' backs.

"What are you playing?" Kimberly asks him.

"Weapons," he says. His younger brother runs up to us too, giggling, and turns around to show us the paper on the back of his thobe: *Uzi,* it says in stark print.

"No you're not," Kimberly says. She peels the paper away and crumples it, and calmly takes her youngest onto her lap when he begins to cry. *"Mom,"* Ahmed says. The mothers are staring openly now; each face is smooth but contemptuous as they look to their own sons now engrossed in their guessing game and back to my daughter-in-law, whose face has grown red from the heat. But then Kimberly stands and directs Ahmed to take up his backpack, and his brother's as well. It's time for lunch and we're going home, she says. Pick up your ghotra and put it on your head, she says to Ahmed. No arguing. She says all this in a perfect stream of Arabic, just a bit more loudly than she needs to, and the mothers watch us as we go, Ahmed scuffing his feet as we pass by the Cadillac where the older boys are smoking now and watching us too.

———

Do you remember? I asked my sister Ghusun. It had been many years since I'd seen her. She moved away with her husband's family when she was thirteen, just a year older than I, and when I saw her after so long I thought I would find her stunted, pressed down by the life she led in a crossroads town where the Great Sands begin. She was darker and rounded but not stunted at all. Her five children —four girls and a boy—played in the rooms behind their father's store while my eldest threw rocks at the animals in the courtyard. Talal was then not yet born. My sister and I hung the wash to dry on the roof and we could see the dunes swelling where the green of the little farms stopped.

Yes yes, she said, *of course I remember.* Oh, all of them—all of them, our three older sisters, like black lumps in a line! They were so quiet. Dull and obedient; barely speaking, hardly moving. I can see them now, Ghusun said: they must be old, they sit in the tent, sad widows, a life of pounding millet and straining laban. No, not a tent, Ghusun—that's over, it's a house now, there are no tents anymore and they are with Omar, because our parents are dead and so he must keep them, our fat hateful brother; they never see anything and they don't want to know. Remember the farm? It was cool there in autumn; the air smelled of dates and our sheep were the plumpest. Yes, but that is gone too. If only Basim—but we will not speak of that brother, we will not speak any more of the dead, no; but why wouldn't he marry, where did he go, remember that boy, the American, that year after the war and why did our brother go off with him? What did it mean? It killed them, you know, our parents—but no, we will not talk of this, this we will not remember, and we are here now and we will talk of other things.

Thurayya, she said, it is good here. The sands roll to the farm; it reminds me of home. This house does not leak and my in-laws are docile. You do not know this, in the city, where they say that the Rub al-Khali brings no life—here it does, you can see, not just *me* and my children but see there, this herd, those camels were born of the ones that came with me. *Your dowry!* I exclaimed. I remember. Yes. So different for me; I wish you'd have seen it. Only money, I said, only that and no herd. But I loved him. So foolish. Don't ask me. Don't ask me.

———

She pushes the T-shirts around in a metal bin, using a spoon from the kitchen. The wood is going blue from the dye. Except for the dress, I look at her and imagine the Golden Gate, sea cupped by cliffs, coconut-oiled legs in fraying denim around a bonfire with boards stuck into the sand. But this is an invention—I have made it from things she has told me.

When I tell her my picture Kimberly laughs and says, "That's good, Thurayya," and I know she is trying to see it herself.

We are here in the desert, all of us, the family. A ritual of sorts: for me it is my first home always—though no goat's wool is needed now to tie up a shelter, and if we see camels they will of course not be ours. Our tent is not as large as my family's was but it has two big rooms, and it is bright blue and shiny and nylon; we could survive in a frost, Talal says, though we will not need to. It is only for one night, and he hopes that the close quarters will bring us—well, close.

We see the boys coming down from the escarpment now with their father. They wave to us and we wave back.

"I had one just like this," Kimberly says, pulling a shirt from the brew. "We made them at camp. You tie the rubber bands on and you get these circles, with little patterns. See?" The boys are wearing Kimberly's old T-shirts today: GO CLIMB A ROCK, and also SHUT YOUR TAP, with a smiling water drop next to a faucet. The things she has kept are from a long time ago.

"It's probably silly," she says. "They just saw tie-dye everywhere in Santa Cruz and decided they loved it."

I am aware that I am indulging her delusion, this frantic activity of hers that is supposed to somehow conjure up a past.

Manar comes out of the tent; she has been napping, away from the sun. Now she calls inside. The four girls come out groggily, Leena last with her marked-up course catalog. She can't decide, she says to no one in particular, whether she should really bother with advanced chemistry because literature would be so much more interesting in the long run. She yawns.

Manar and Kimberly exchange looks; for a moment they almost laugh.

Now the boys are back. Kimberly corrals them while Manar scans the distance for Talal, who is nowhere to be seen. Ahmed says he is hungry. "I made tabbouleh," Kimberly says, "and it'll have to hold us till dinner's ready. Amdi, get your grandma some juice."

Ahmed pokes at the blue shirts drying on a line in the wind.

"Juice," Manar reminds him, with a small push on the shoulder. "Don't keep Grandma waiting. It's still hot out. And Leena—" But the girl has wandered off, stretching her arms out of her loose cotton sleeves, ridding herself of her sighs before she finds her father. She will sit and talk with him while the men roast the sheep in its pit. We will be the picture of serenity when they return. My place on the big rug is always with my back to the tent, Talal across from me, the three little girls quietly around their mother and Kimberly with her two sons, Leena flitting.

"You can have it later," Kimberly says to Ahmed now. "Wait till it's all dry."

She goes to the cooler in the back of the Land Rover and gets drinks for everyone, handing me mine first, lemonade in a glass decorated with fish.

"Is that all right?" Manar asks me. She takes the pitcher from Kimberly and her lips reach into a smile. "Or did you want something else?"

———

Leena is speaking urgently to her father, who zips his jacket up to his neck. When it is spring and the nights are cool in the desert Talal never wants his thobe, although he keeps his headdress on: tonight the red-checked ghotra clashes with the green Adidas tracksuit and he looks like a mismatched jockey. "It's fine, it's fine," he says to Leena. She wants him to know how serious she is. She will *not* become frivolous because then she won't be accepted at the School of Art, or maybe the Conservatory, anyway it is so competitive out there, these days. She is fourteen and very certain that she is creative. Talal winks at me and when Leena catches this she pouts a little, but she is probably sure she'll have her way.

"You have a long time, Leena," I say. "Years and years. When I was your age I was supposed to be married."

Talal gathers sand in his fist and lets it slowly sift out.

"I know," Leena says.

She can't imagine.

"Don't worry, *habib*," Talal says and hugs her. "You can do as you like."

Leena smiles but she's looking at me.

I watch the fire go down.

———

Not strange to think of money—what a riyal is to an ounce of gold, or how this mutation, from animal to coin to self, is one I can remember. In my village I watched my sisters, when I was young, their limbs weighed down by bracelets as they left with their husbands. My father had so many sheep and camels we scarcely noticed what we'd been given and what we'd given away. Only the sisters returned, deaths and misfortune to blame—they had to. When the man I married came for me we went to the city and when

138

our sons chose their brides we said *cash*, cash would never be used. This was modern. These days, a daughter with aspirations has a value you calculate otherwise. Still you know: what you are worth in a deal, whatever is traded, whatever passes through handshakes. You know there is something you will need to offer in return.

———

A wedding: my son's. The halls of the Intercontinental Hotel teemed with families and friends: the men dined upstairs in the penthouse, while the women waited in the great hall for hours. The little girls mussed their long dresses and chased the youngest boys. In the clamor of the hall the chasing passed for supervision; while the women gossiped and rustled in their finery, the girls ran and jumped and dove under chairs. Their screechings went unchecked. Older girls danced to the drums, whipping their hair around and around to the rhythm. Their eyes shone as they held hands and they appraised this one's jewels, or that one's; at a wedding like this, you wondered who would be next. The old women passed incense while the dancing girls took breaks and sipped lemon water from iced pitchers. The wedding party showed themselves twice: Manar's ornate tribal gown with the gold coins and chains drew exclamations from the older women and her white dress, which was French, was admired by the girls. She was gone with a toss of her veil, with Talal in her wake. Now the women could eat. A city wedding, both proper and modern—all could approve. Later, at the more intimate gatherings that would last until dawn, the married women reclined in small salons and talked frankly about what brides didn't know, while the dancing girls—still dancing now, but to pop music on CDs—compared kissings and gropings from vacations abroad and guessed at who might be betrayed if bridal sheets were still used for display.

Another wedding. This time the bride in one dress, layers of flounced yellow cotton, its length undecided between knee and ankle. A veil pinned to her light hair with flowers. Pushing her sleeves up to her elbows in the bathroom, awkwardly because they had been added for coverage—*all right,* she said to herself in the mirror. *Let's do this.* Not fifty people at the Intercontinental that day; we had booked the family section, so the men and women ate at the same tables and the children, feeling important, had their own table and waiter. The men were Saudis, just into their thirties, with their wives. Kimberly's friends were not so many as you would think: only four of them, young American women with bright eye shadow who chattered with one another and smoked cigarettes. Some men who knew her father. Manar held court at her own table; she came away only to fix Kimberly's dress or pin her veil back into her hair. Kimberly's father smoked a cigar with Talal out on the hotel balcony and looked below at the limousines circling into the courtyard. We were waiting to see if Talal's older brother Alim would come. We waited. When Kimberly kissed her father goodbye he held onto her hand. A few hours later Manar passed fresh mint with sugar cubes to the women sitting on cushions in her receiving room, and she looked as rosy as the shell-colored walls. *It's perfect,* she said. The small group of women smiled brightly—so modern, oh so modern. They did not know how to contradict her. But they imagined it. *Too modern.* And as for Kimberly, now what?

—

Alim, unfortunately, is also my son. His wives are pious and sit in their rooms like women from another age, terrified and silent. They remind me of my sisters: useless. Though I suppose I would have to define *useful* to condemn them like that. When my husband died Alim was head of the family, and he organized our assets and issued decrees. He raged that we had to be respectable. He ordered Talal to take another wife who would give him sons. Manar made a run to Jeddah and Alim had her arrested; he threatened to keep all of our passports. I refused him mine and instructed the concierge in the towers not to buzz him in. Being an old woman has its uses, with authority.

Manar met Kimberly when they were both in jail—Kimberly having finally run out of her expat luck with an arrest for possessing contraband. There they made their deal that was to allow them

both to win: Kimberly would avoid deportation by marrying Talal
—for she knew no other country as her home—and Manar could
get back at Alim. Talal would divorce Kimberly and leave her with
satisfactory assets and citizenship. Did they truly think it would all
happen? When it did, this American wife—and her father, the
drunken fool, dead now too—were what finally sent Alim and his
family packing to Yanbu.

What I mean is that he gave us up.

And Manar had been overconfident, about what she thought
was hers.

Maybe there is something I love about complications. There
are issues to settle here—and I am the one, in this family now, who
does so. When Talal married Manar I was proud; I had approved
her, I had known her, it was right. The trick we played on Alim
with Kimberly was designed to tame him. Then their faces, that day
at the wedding: it was done. And I could not explain why something about those sleeves—they wouldn't stay up—and that veil—
cheap and flimsy; how it touched me. It touched me and I shifted,
and I loved her, like that.

———

Do you remember? I asked her. Now we were older, Ghusun and
I, and more things had changed. We sat in her courtyard where
wind stirred the palms; with water priced higher, the leaves cracked
in the sun and the trunks were parched. Our sleep in the night had
been heated. Many years now, again—the children were grown. I
told her of the wailing of air raid sirens in Riyadh, the boom and
flash of missiles, debris falling like flaming stars. She closed her eyes
against the sound of trucks that churned through the village in a
never-ending caravan. It was still an outpost, but with little green
left. Food and gasoline came with the trucks and were bought again
by others passing through.

Yes, she said slowly. Tell me again. How does it work, with
this American girl—how is it different? Do people talk? They still
do, I said, though she now has a son. There, hah!—there's tradition,
Ghusun said. No man wants only daughters, not *mine* nor your son,

when my boy died then *she* came, see how it is now. You were lucky. You never knew the one your husband went to; you didn't see her, she wasn't there. I said, *No.* She rose up—I remember—thin from the pain that grasped her. She moved bent and careful, then gathered her dress in a hand as she scanned the closed doors around the courtyard. In the dead dust of that place she suddenly shone there like fire. The other woman's children we could hear but not see; their laughter bounced from inside the walls. It wavered and multiplied in a taunting echo.

Look at us, she said. Old now. It's too late; we know too much. And for whom to be sorry? For *her,* or for him? For your son, or the two who live with him? But not for ourselves. No, not that. And I wanted to help but could not; there we were again together, time gone by us, and the Quarter pushed its sands to her home as if to swallow it, as if to feed on the life she had remaining to sustain the new.

———

And now they are playing it out for me. After a night of sleep the boys are ravenous; they want eggs with harissa, hot sauce to burn their tongues so they can cool them with orange juice straight from the container. Kimberly cooks on a grill over the fire and they eat from metal containers that expand and collapse like telescopes. Today the three all wear tie-dyed shirts with their jeans. They sit cross-legged on prayer rugs, and Ahmed exclaims that his younger brother stinks—they have not had baths since the day before last. Fifty feet away from the tent they are their own little camp.

On the rise behind us Talal makes his way down from the escarpment. His hands are in the pockets of his tracksuit and he looks behind him as he pushes his feet into the soft grains of the slope. He has been away for over an hour—by now the sun seems as if it is chasing him, looming from the edge of the cliff and over.

With the girls there is talk of going earlier than planned, because when it gets hotter they will have to deal with the flies, a battle with no end. The younger girls watch Manar dictating to the maid what they will have to eat: just croissants, with jelly, and fruit. Manar wears an expensive version of a Bedouin dress—purple silk with embroidery lacing across the chest, swirling around her hem. I think of strong cotton: colors deep as crushed dates and richer than anything that shines.

Leena says she wants to drive the Land Rover before we leave. Her father promised, so we will be staying for another hour. Manar frowns as Leena goes over to the other fire to tell the boys they will have a ride.

When Talal is closer he looks at both little clusters of his family, and I know he is deciding which way to go first. He stops some yards away and lights a cigarette, blowing smoke into the air.

———

There is a shrill buzz from the intercom and the concierge says that my American daughter-in-law is here. You can hear it in his voice, though he is very polite: *this* daughter-in-law.

As a Pakistani he would not express his disapproval of me, a woman living alone. But he will say, how is your son, madame? I hope that he will be visiting you again soon.

"I'm sorry it's so early," Kimberly says.

She takes off her abayah and piles it in a heap on my counter. Her veil takes a minute to unwind because the bobby pins catch in her hair. This is when she looks most comfortable with herself, peeling away one layer as if she's discovering the next.

"Well, then sorry about the mess," I say. "I'll make tea."

"No, that's fine, you know I can hardly say anything about that." She thumbs through my stack of magazines. "Thurayya," she laughs, "since when do you read *Vogue?*"

"Leena's," I say. "She has her sources already."

"I'll say. The other day I heard her talking to one of her friends in Zurich, giving her a list of magazines to bring back in her luggage. They're just not afraid."

"You weren't afraid," I remind her.

She shrugs. "No, I didn't care," she says. "We always thought we'd be excused, anyway."

I notice her tan seems faded. While I brew the tea she settles into the chair by the window, looking out to the balcony and the skyline she knows so well. She flips through the magazine; the pictures seem to mesmerize her, and now and then she smiles hesitantly, as if in wonderment. I pour the tea into large glasses so I won't have to get up to refill, and when I hand one to her she says, "You know, I think I'd feel like I was pretending with all this—anywhere." She gestures with the magazine, flicking the pages, as if to say, *this*.

I know it's not quite what she means. In a different way from Manar, she too has grown cautious. She's always had two lives; now the one she's tried so hard to subsume is making its absence known, making her unsure.

"It's about as new-fashioned as it gets," she said to me once. "It's not like I didn't know." This was about a year after she married Talal. The war was over, and Ahmed had been born. We let him roll and gurgle on a sheet on my living-room floor while we talked about the new business deals between Talal and her father, and Kimberly joked that she had managed to hold up her end of the bargain, much to her surprise.

Now she says, "I think I'm going to have to leave for a while. Maybe—I don't know. I need to take six months and see what happens."

"Talal does love you," I say.

"I know, Thurayya, I know." She twists her glass in her hands. "And believe me—for a long time I was just grateful. I thought I belonged here, and it seemed like the right way to do it. There weren't supposed to be children. We could have gotten a divorce."

"Yes," I say. "You could have."

"But we didn't."

"No."

"And now, he thinks we should. We aren't talking any more. We're all just focusing on the children, and Talal, and Manar, and

144

me—we don't have any idea. We're just stuck and nobody remembers anymore why any of this happened. We're this close"—she holds up her thumb and index finger, with a tiny space in between—"to hating one another."

She takes a breath, expels it.

I ask her if she knows what she wants. She says that she can see herself still happy here, but of course there is Manar to consider. Perhaps she needs to spend some time in the country where she was born—where she hardly grew up, a place she does not know. She kicks at the magazine, now lying open on the floor beside her, and says that she does not even know *that*, and it is not the things she covets, it's the knowledge of where it comes from. "I don't even know my own mother," she says. "She's been in California all these years, since way before I came here with my father. I've seen her, maybe, five times since I was eight years old."

"Then you need to do it," I tell her.

"The boys need to know her too," she says. "Even if only a little. She's their grandmother too." This softly, looking at me, like an apology.

Together we watch the sun climbing toward noon, looking through the glass and not talking.

"Did you know that I blame myself for Alim?" I ask her after awhile. When she looks skeptical I say, "No, it's true. When he was a boy I convinced myself that I had everything I needed here in Riyadh, everything new, and I thought I was so happy to be away from my family and that life that I never went back. Not even when my sisters died, one by one, and then there was no one I knew in that village."

I crush more sugar into my glass, making it syrupy, and tell her more. "But my husband never forgot the woman he was supposed to marry—she died." I pause, remembering, and thinking of Ghusun's words: *You were lucky,* she said. "He did not love me. Not when he married me, nor later. He was angry. There was no respect. And I did not complain; by doing everything he asked I could get him to leave me alone, and I had other things. Books, for instance—my brother Basim taught me to read as a child, and so I got better at it. But Alim, he learned how to live from his father."

"Talal isn't like that," Kimberly says, and there's a spark of loyalty in her voice.

"By the time Talal was born my husband had left us, more or less. There was no divorce, and we had enough money—he simply lived away from us, with his mistresses. Talal hardly knew him. My husband arranged Alim's marriage and his affairs, but Talal was on his own."

"He abandoned a *son?*" Kimberly asks. Our biases here have seeped into her.

"He thought Talal weak," I say. At this she and I both look suddenly guilty.

"I am telling you that I gave one son up to his father. To protect the other." And I am thinking now: how can I protect him again, when it is more complicated? There are no villains this time.

"My sister Ghusun—" I start to tell her this too, but I stop. Kimberly's legs are curled under her in the chair now; lit up by the window's glow, she looks tentative still, but she smiles at me. "We'll make plans," I tell her. When what remains is family, it cannot be saved in the ways we used to do it. We have ourselves to think of, as well.

———

My talking makes Kimberly restless, she says—so we call Saudi Limousine and ride down to the souks by the clock tower. Years ago, when I arrived as a bride, there were only rugs on the ground and vendors shaded themselves under canopies, their camels tied to hitches in a row behind them. The sound of prayer call from the mosque would start the animals braying. *Zhuhr* was the worst time to shop, and you went then only if you had to; noon's heat drove the stench to its zenith, and the honking din of the camels rattled your head.

Now the limousine curves through a parking lot to let us off. There's still noise—the driver taps on his horn even when we're idling—but the smells are different, gasoline and exhaust and the sweat of people who have been perfumed. We're after the old, as much as one can get these days: behind the new shops and stalls and through winding corridors we catch a lonely scent, a trail of cheap sandalwood and grease that seems to have bloomed and staled for centuries. The shops on these alleyways are hidden from view. "Like Sleeping Beauty's castle, frozen in time," Kimberly whispers as we go more slowly now, the sounds of the world we came from fading away. An ancient Sudanese woman, balancing a washtub of soda cans and ice on her head, waddles around a corner, trailed by a raggedy cat. At a small shop we find prayer rugs small enough for children. They're dusty and forlorn. Kimberly says her mother will use them under flowerpots, or maybe just to sit on the porch stairs, where the beach sends up sand. There are rows of brass coffee urns and palm-sized water pipes in a smudged glass display case. We still have these things today, but they are made new and shiny; we wonder who buys these relics. The shopkeeper loads us up with plastic bags.

We're still wandering when afternoon prayer comes and we sit close together on a stoop and get our hands sticky from warm soda cans. Kimberly sorts through her bags and laughs at the prayer rugs we've bought, the cheap weaves and garish patterns nothing one of us would own.

"My mother deserves these," she says when I ask why she chose them.

I think I am helping.

———

Manar has left a message on my machine when I return. When I call back I get Leena instead, who says her mother is out—she doesn't say where.

I ask her to come visit me on the weekend. Grandmother's advice.

Now it is I who am restless.

Our lives have been constructed: where we can go and what we are permitted to do, rituals upheld and upended from mother to daughter as we work our way around our men. It is the same today as it has been always—with refinements. A school in Switzerland is the equivalent milestone to my learning letters from words printed on postcards almost fifty years ago.

And our endless competitions and maneuverings continue the threat of undoing, when we decide that our disappointments outweigh the risk of bestowing freedom where we should.

———

"Leave it to me," I say when Kimberly calls again later.

She is distraught and has been crying, and when I tell her that I will come she says *all right.* Talal is away on business for the week and she has decided to leave before he returns. Manar has taken the boys' passports and locked them in her safe and is threatening to contact Alim.

An inevitable irony, I think.

I call a driver to pick me up. It is late now, and the young men with nothing to do are cruising in long lines in their cars, honking and braking to talk with their windows rolled down in the cooled air. Once through the tangled cloverleaf of roads surrounding the towers, we soar onto the flyover like a night bird. A rush of possibility you suck in like a breeze every time you do it. We pass curtained windows rising from behind walled villas. Lights and movement flicker from the edges and everything is straining to stay in.

Instead of waiting, I push through the front door of Talal's house. Because the houseboy doesn't have time to announce me, I surprise Manar watching television with the sound turned off. She is alone in her sitting room, looking defiant on a long couch that curves around the wall.

She looks at me with angry eyes and runs the lacquered nails of one hand over the palm of the other. Behind the doors down the hallway I can sense waiting. I sit across from her and look back at her just as hard, giving her the chance to admit how ridiculous and poisonous her game is.

"Why are you helping her?" she asks, not disguising her bitterness.

"Because I want her to come back," I tell her.

"I see," Manar says coolly, "that you are now choosing a wife for your son."

She twists a fold of her dress and pulls on it, her mouth tightening. I say that Talal is confused and she laughs like a whip cracking—because this is the truth she neglected, and what she should have known about him when she arranged for this to happen eight years ago.

My daughter-in-law, the one by all laws of heritage I should be siding with but am not, pulls herself straight and away from me. She says that it is Kimberly who should leave—alone. "I admit to it," she says. "I brought her into my house. It was my doing."

"You've always owned up to it," I say.

"Yes, I have. And there would be no sons but for me." Now she's up and pacing furiously, defiant. "Maybe," she says, "Alim was right."

"Stop, Manar. You don't know what you mean."

"No?" she says. "Don't I? Oh, God——" She turns away and presses her hands over her face. A deep breath, ragged, and then she holds herself rigid, holds herself in. "What would you have done?" she asks finally. "What would you have done?"

"You can't keep the boys," I tell her, gently but firm.

"I know," she says. Now her voice is quavering, uncertain. She nods her head mechanically.

I take her hand in mine and she repeats "I know, I know," as I hold it. Kimberly will go, I tell her, and the boys will go with her. Leena will leave for Switzerland and before she goes Manar and Talal will spend time with her, just with her, as they prepare her for her new life away from home. Tell her what it means, I say, that though she may be veiled here, it does not mean that she should behave as if she is veiled when she is there. You must trust her, I say.

"And Kimberly——"

"We don't know," I say. "We can't. You must all make up your minds, and so we are making these separations now, so you can breathe. He won't do it himself."

Manar examines me with a trace of a smile. She looks around the room for a moment, taking in the dusky blue of this year's walls and the ribbons of brocade running down in silvery stripes. The television flickers. Running her fingers along the edge of a velvet cushion, as if for reassurance, she says: "Talal will be angry."

"At first," I say. "Yes."

The truth is that he will have been outnumbered, in the way that the weak can be.

—

My sister died in the city. When it happened—and she knew it was going to happen, not needing any diagnosis to tell her—she asked her husband to allow her to pass quickly, at home. From the rooftop she could see the village and imagine where she would be buried. Her husband agreed, solicitous now. Then his relatives came to pay their final respects and they told him what a disgrace it was, leaving a first wife to repine like that when modern medicine could make her more comfortable. They'd become city people, but they remained superstitious: a home death might bring bad luck. The younger wife, wanting to look good, agreed with them. And so Ghusun was driven more than two hundred miles to Al-Hufuf, over her protestations, to a hospital where a European doctor confirmed what she already knew to be true. She lived her last days in a white room, her bed surrounded by a blue curtain. There were no windows. The bleating of electronic machines kept her awake. This she told me, from the telephone at her bedside, while we waited together across the distance and told stories to one another once more.

—

Here is what Ghusun recalled.

She recounted that summer when everything changed—when we were children still, after that second time the world had gone to war, that summer when our brother Basim brought home the American boy, when they disappeared into the desert and we never saw them again. We were daughters. We had been fortunate: until then it seemed we might live out lives other than those expected of us. After Basim was gone there was shame on my family, and to appease it Ghusun agreed to be married. She had been my close companion. Did I ask her to make such a sacrifice? We both knew that her early marriage would have some extreme effect on my future. It turned out to be an advantage.

There are small ways time turns: a brother who leaves with a soldier, a son with two worlds under his roof. A granddaughter who might at last make that leap forward, taking with her both the old and the new. These are ways to travel, and they are inevitable—if we let them be. Though perhaps where I am is twenty stories up on some road that goes nowhere.

On the evening when Kimberly leaves I look out of my window and imagine the distance to the Empty Quarter, the Rub al-Khali, and hold a magazine in my lap. I flip through the pictures of vineyards and picnics and coastal highways I've never seen and run my fingers over the captions of words I don't know how to translate.

———

I think that no one has ever done it, despite what the stories say.

As children Ghusun and I played a game whenever one of the elder sisters returned home. We pranced around each other outside the tent and said, giggling, *I divorce you, I divorce you, I divorce you.*

Three times, is the rule.

I divorce you.

Though if it is the woman who wishes it, she is supposed to have witnesses, and it is mathematics of female to male. Three voices, balanced like weights: who will stay, who will go, how you leave.

ACKNOWLEDGMENTS

This book was written with the generous support of the Fine Arts Work Center in Provincetown, the Jentel Artist Residency Program, the Edward F. Albee Foundation, the MacDowell Colony, and the Writing Program at Washington University in St. Louis.

I'm grateful also for the Virginia refuge provided by Kris, Chris, and Emelie Boucher, and Bob and Linda Claymier.

Some of these stories have been previously published: "Pioneer" in *Shenandoah*, "The Date Farm" in *Other Voices*, "Slow Stately Dance in Triple Time" in *Dossier*, "Hayloader" in *Crab Orchard Review*, "Safety" in *Kenyon Review*, and "Rub al-Khali" in *Malahat Review*. My thanks to the editors of these journals for their support and suggestions. I also want to thank Ann Patchett and the staff at the University of Pittsburgh Press for making it all come together.

For superlative editorial advice I owe thanks to Joshua Henkin, Marshall Klimasewiski, Matthew Korfhage, Hilary Mantel, Rob Phelps, Heidi Jon Schmidt, David Schuman, Salvatore Scibona, Emily Shelton, Roger Skillings, Kellie Wells, and Thomas Yagoda. And a special mention to Jim Dalglish for *becoming* one of my characters. He has since recovered.